Ponderfoot's Dollars

Jack Barley's problems are many: the bank is about to foreclose on his farm and the local community treat his family as pariahs. However, the threat that arrives in the shape of the notorious outlaw Bannion brothers brings the biggest problem yet.

The Bannions are on their way to rob the local bank, but tracked by a deadly U.S. marshal they hit upon a scheme to avoid danger to themselves. They will get Jack to rob the bank in return for his wife and son's safety.

Jack goes through with their demands, but with the marshal getting suspicious and the money gone missing can he save his family?

By the same author

Kirk's Law
Ruben's Ruse
Robb's Stand
Hangman's Lot
Flint's Bounty
Fast Gun Range
Rope Justice

Ponderfoot's Dollars

Ben Coady

ROBERT HALE · LONDON

First published in Great Britain 2006

ISBN-10: 0-7090-7961-3
ISBN-13: 978-0-7090-7961-3

Robert Hale Limited
Clerkenwell House
Clerkenwell Green
London EC1R 0HT

Typeset by Derek Doyle & Associates, Shaw Heath.
Printed and bound in Great Britain by
Antony Rowe Limited, Wiltshire

CHAPTER ONE

'Riders coming, Pa!'

Jack Barley paused from forking hay to look to where his boy was pointing to the hills behind the barn at the three men coming from a wooded slope, immediate anxiety showing in his grey eyes. The Civil War was still a raw memory, and for many a festering sore, particularly those men who had worn the grey of the Confederacy who could not accept the South's defeat, and these men fitted a saddle with a military gait. They could be Union or Reb. But at a guess, the latter. If that were so, then the chances were that they came with bitter baggage.

On the Union side, too, there were men who bore grudges and those who figured that the only acceptable outcome to the war was the total humiliation of the South. In fact, if those men had their way, there would be a new order of slavery, and those slaves would be the men who had fought for the Confederacy.

For the men on both sides of the divide, the war was still being fought in the small towns, saloons and open range. Sometimes with guns, fists and boots. Other times by the more sly means of outcasting and humiliation. Whatever means were adopted, the end result was a legacy of hatred and anger that, Jack Barley reckoned, would take his and a lifetime more to eradicate. There were cankers of poison in bitter hearts that would take a generation if not longer to assuage. And there was one other type of man who was despised by both sides; the man who had by conviction of faith or character rejected both sides: the pacifist.

Jack Barley, a devout Quaker, was such a man. And a long time ago, he had learned that pacifism and cowardice were one and the same to most men.

On hearing her son's summons to his father, Ellie Barley had come from the house dusting flour from her hands, her anxiety about the three riders every bit as acute as her husband's.

'Best stay in the house, Ellie,' Barley said. 'You too, Sammy.'

The instruction did not go down well with the boy. At ten years of age, he figured that he was old enough not to be sent packing every time there was a hint of danger and menace. In his childish way, he understood his pa's struggle to hold on to the farm when his produce was rejected by the town stores and the agents who went round the territory acting for the big buyers of grain and crops. And recently he had overheard a conversation between Charles Archer the town's bank president and his pa about matters he did not fully understand, like those strange words fluidity and mortage. But he knew instinctively that the gloom left behind by the banker's visit was not a good feeling, and that Archer's visit meant trouble. This had been confirmed when he had woken in the night and had heard his ma crying in the quiet way a woman does when all hope is gone.

'We'll be OK,' he had heard his pa say, through the thin wall separating his bedroom from his parents. But it was a tired and weary reassurance that gave his ma no comfort, because she had kept on weeping.

'I can help, Pa,' Sammy Barley said, his eyes a match of his pa's, full of determination.

'Sure you can, Sammy,' Jack Barley said, his smile kind despite the burden of worry that hunched his shoulders. He ruffled the boy's fairish hair, which would probably lighten to the blonde of Ellie Barley's, sweeping back his fringe with his fingers into the natural kink, like his mother's, that curled his fringe back behind his right ear. 'But I'd feel a whole lot more comforted if I knew that there was a man in the house. Your ma needs caring for.'

Sammy's eyes beamed. 'You figure, Pa?'

'I figure, Sammy. Now take your ma inside the house.'

He looked beyond the boy to Ellie, his look sad and hopeless. Ellie Barley forced back the rush of tears as Sammy came towards the house dragging his left leg. Broken by a mule kick the year before, it had set badly. She did not know how long their suffering would go on for, with crops rotting in the ground, mortgage repayments overdue, and Jack having to suffer slur after slur from men only a smidgen of his worth.

Sometimes, more and more in recent times, she had begun to question her husband's pacifist stand. She was not a Quaker, and could not fully understand the religious belief that drove him. But there were and had been days when she had wished that he had gone to war like other men. Maybe he would have died, but his death by shot and shell would have been mercifully quick. Rather than the slow death he was now enduring day by day. She had learned that there were many ways a man could die, and the worst way of all was to be still breathing but dead inside. That was a cruelty and an injustice that Jack Barley did not deserve, and at times she could not help herself hating God for demanding so much of him.

'Pa says that I'm to take care of you in the house, Ma,' Sammy said proudly. 'Says you need caring for.'

Ellie gathered Sammy to her. 'Sure I do, Sammy. With a man with me, I'll feel a whole lot safer.' She drew him into the house.

'Now, while your pa is talking to those men, I'm sure that we can find something useful to do.'

'I ain't making no apple pies, Ma,' Sammy declared. 'That ain't man's work.'

'Of course it isn't, honey. No. What I want you to do is go into the parlour and keep watch from the window, and holler in good time if the men are coming to the house.' Her hands swept her apron. 'That'll give me time to make myself presentable and not disgrace your pa.'

'Heck, Ma,' Sammy groaned. 'You look pretty as a picture right now.'

Ellie laughed and kissed Sammy on the forehead.

'I swear, young Sammy Barley, that with a tongue as slick as yours, one day you'll break a thousand hearts.'

'Shucks, Ma,' Sammy said as she clung to him.

'You're getting real soppy now.'

'The parlour, young man,' she ordered playfully.

Once Sammy had entered the room, she closed the parlour door and hurried to the rear of the hall where a rifle hung on the wall, held fast by a piece of string around its barrel, looking pristine because it had only been fired once in the six years it had hung there, and that was to scare off a coyote worrying the hen house. It would probably not function, or blow up if it did, and she hated the feel of the weapon in her hands. But, grimly determined, she took the rifle and went to the kitchen window from where she could monitor the riders' approach, not at all sure of what she could do, if anything needed doing. If there was trouble, all she could hope for was to scare the men away. Shooting them would take skill which she had not got.

Jack Barley stood and waited for the men, not liking one bit their cocky gait. They were men who had spent a whole lot of time in the saddle, and that probably meant that they were men who roamed looking for trouble or dodging what little law the territory had.

As they drew nearer, he could see their hard faces. And as they came closer still, their equally hard eyes. Two of the men flanked the leader, hanging behind in his shadow, eyes never at rest.

As they entered the yard they distanced themselves further from the lead rider, and drifted off to either side to outflank Barley.

The men having passed out of sight of the kitchen window, Ellie left the house to take up a position at the side of the house. The rifle shook in her hands.

The leader rode towards Jack Barley, sure of himself, obviously not figuring on any trouble.

'Howdy,' he greeted amiably. The man's tone marked him as Southerner, probably Tennessee. 'Kindly weather we're havin', ain't it?'

Barley nodded. 'It's surely a gift from God, sir.' He chuckled and looked to the dark rolling clouds to the south. 'Though He might be about to change His mind. Storm coming, I reckon.'

'My pards and me are feelin' a little parched. Wonder if you'd mind us fillin' our canteens from your well.'

'It's right behind me,' Barley said, pointing over his left shoulder.

'That's mighty friendly and obligin', mister,' one of the other men said, plainly the youngest of the three.

'I try to be neighbourly,' Barley said.

'Fill your canteens, boys,' the leader said.

The men dismounted and strode past Barley on their way to the well. He felt uncomfortable with them behind him, but were he to turn and look it would alert them to his nervousness. And in country where a man's stance was often the difference between living and dying, Jack Barley knew that he had to give the impression of a man who could, if called upon, defend himself. These men were probably just a notch above wild animals and, like a wild animal, would pounce on a scent of fear. However, in reality he was probably not fooling anyone but himself, but there was little else he could do but bluff and hope that once their canteens were replenished they would ride on.

He had not missed the leader's shifty glances assessing the farm's worth, and Barley was pleased by the man's obvious low calculation of pickings to be found. For once, Barley was glad that he did not have the trappings of affluence that would tempt these men. Dirt farmer as penniless as a church mouse was the message in the leader's eyes.

He had nothing worth killing him for.

That was when Jack Barley spotted Ellie at the side of the house. When the men at the well filling their canteens turned round, they would see her.

Now there was something worth killing for.

CHAPTER TWO

'The name's Howie Bannion,' the leader of the trio announced. 'You work this farm on your ownsome, mister?'

'I've got a couple of men about somewhere,' Barley bluffed, swallowing hard. He had heard of Howie Bannion. The other men riding with him had to be Dan and Ike Bannion. The trio formed the Bannion Brothers – outlaws who took what they wanted when they wanted, and never allowed anyone to stand in their way when doing so.

'Yeah?' There was a mocking snigger in Howie Bannion's voice. 'We ain't seen no one.'

'They're around,' Barley said.

'Family man?'

'You ask a lot of questions, Mr Bannion. The answer to your question is no. This isn't the place for a man to have family.'

Bannion seemed satisfied with that answer.

'Must be kinda lonely,' he observed.

'Haven't got time to be lonely. Farming takes up a lot of a man's time.'

'My pa was a sodbuster. Kept turnin' the sod 'til it killed him. Now, me, well I figgered that sodbustin' wasn't for me.'

Jack Barley shrugged. 'You love it or hate it.'

'I guess that's a fact an' all,' Howie Bannion agreed, and called out: 'Hey, fellas, you goin' to drain that well dry?'

'Comin', Howie,' the taller of the duo and the older of the pair at the well called back, without turning round.

Closer in age to Howie Bannion would make him Ike Bannion.

Barley had taken the brief opportunity offered by Howie Bannion's attention on his brothers to shift his stance slightly to put him sideways to the outlaw leader. He waved a hand behind his back to send a signal to Ellie to get back inside the house. But all there was time for was a fleeting gesture that she might or might not see and might or might not interpret correctly. He would have to live through the hellish seconds when the men at the well turned round to find out if his desperate signal to Ellie had worked or not, because he could not risk checking for fear of alerting the outlaws to her presence.

'Those fellas 'round are takin' their sweet time in showin' themselves, ain't they?' Howie Bannion said. 'I figgered that they'd have come runnin' when we showed up. Just in case we were trouble callin'.'

'This is a pretty peaceful neck of the woods,' Barley said.

Barley gripped the pitchfork he had been forking hay with, his knuckles made white by the intensity of his grip. It was the only weapon he had to hand. Howie Bannion's slight shift of gaze was not lost on Barley. He had spotted the sudden tension in his grip on the pitch fork.

'Wind's pickin' up,' he said conversationally. He sniffed the air. 'Rain on the way, I reckon.'

Barley shook his head like a man with a lot of problems. 'Rain will be surely welcome after the long dry spell we've had.'

'Yeah. My old man used to wear out his kneecaps praying for rain that mostly never came.' He chuckled. 'And when it did, there was too much of it anyway.'

Jack Barley laughed along with the outlaw, hoping to humour him. 'There should be some kind of magic wand that a sodbuster could wave to turn it on and off as he pleased.'

'Hey now, wouldn't that be somethin' real handy.' Howie Bannion waved an imaginary wand in the air. 'Rain.' Then he waved the imaginary wand again. 'No rain.'

Their canteens filled, Dan and Ike Bannion made to return to their horses. Jack Barley's heart staggered. However, unconcerned, the outlaws mounted up. Barley silently thanked the Almighty. Obviously Ellie had understood him. With any luck the Bannions would be on their way. Then Howie Bannion dismounted and went to the well to fill his canteen, prolonging Barley's torture. Seconds hung heavy in the air, each one weighing on Barley's shoulders. The outlaw leader slugged from his replenished canteen. His lazy pose against the well did not match his busy eyes. What was he waiting for? Why the hell didn't he mount up and ride on? Jack Barley figured he knew why. He hadn't yet made up his mind if there was anything worth taking. Or maybe anyone? Had he perhaps seen Ellie? It was possible. Howie Bannion had the kind of eyes that did not miss much. A fly flicking his wing on a saloon mirror would be seen by Howie Bannion.

He rubbed his belly.

'Kinda hollow,' he said. 'You wouldn't have any spare grub in the house, would ya?' Panic raced through Jack Barley, and he felt a cold sweat break on his back.

CHAPTER THREE

'Sorry. I need all I've got, Mr Bannion,' Jack Barley said, gambling on a direct approach being best. At least that left no room for argument, and left the move up to the outlaw.

'Hey, Howie,' Ike Bannion said, 'Ain't that a mite unfriendly?'

'I'd say,' Dan Bannion, the youngest of the Bannion brothers joined in, and if stories were true, the meanest. It was said that he had long ago run out of space for anymore notches on his gun.

Howie Bannion nodded his head in agreement with his brothers' views. 'A man alone don't need much,' he said.

Barley wondered now if he might have played a different hand. Perhaps he should have invited them into the house and been sociable. But then he'd have to gamble on the Bannions' attitude to Ellie. Men who rode long and hard trails, forced by pursuit of one kind or another to spend lengthy spells away from towns where saloon women could satisfy their needs, often got woman fever. And when that happened, a woman did not have to be as pretty or as well proportioned as Ellie Barley was to excite them. Inside the house he might have stood a better chance if trouble flared. Out in the open, he might sink the pitchfork in the Bannion a handle length away, but that would leave the other two Bannions to deliver certain death. Then Ellie and Sammy would be at their mercy, and mercy was not a virtue that the Bannion Bothers were noted for.

'So what d'ya reckon we should do about it, Howie?' Ike asked.

'Now, Brothers,' Howie Bannion began with false placation, 'a man's got a right to be unfriendly if he wants to be. So I figure that we should mosey along and leave this man in peace.'

'Huh?' Dan Bannion yelped, obviously astonished by his older brother's attitude.

However, though Howie Bannion's words were placatory, Jack Barley had not missed the hard glint in his eyes that was as deadly as snake poison. He strode to his horse, turning the mare before mounting up. The slick, barely noticeable move, hid his gun hand from view. Barley was about to lunge at Dan Bannion who was closest, when Ike Bannion said, 'Howie.'

Howie Bannion looked towards the house. Barley, too. A man was standing on the porch holding a rifle, his stance still casual but ready to be confrontational if that was what was called for. Barley had to work hard to keep his astonishment from showing. Ellie had dressed in his clothes and was posing as a work hand. The only explanation that sprang to mind was that she must have heard him bluff the Bannions about men being around, and had decided to pose as one – mighty effectively too, if a man's scrutiny was not too close. Ellie was a tall woman, and her body had become hard from the intensive labour of farming.

Joining in the ruse, Barley called out, 'Are Bob and Hal around, Ben? That fence we were talking about at supper last evening is still unmended.'

Ellie pointed over her shoulder to indicate the men's presence to the rear of the house. So far the Bannions seemed to have been fooled. But for how long? He needed to get Ellie out of sight, before the outlaws saw that even the loosley fitting work clothes could not fully disguise the shape of womanly hips.

'Well, I guess it can wait until tomorrow. Go

tell them to wash up for supper. And maybe come and meet our visitors first.'

Ellie waved and went back inside the house. Barley noted the quick eye messages passing between the brothers, but was not sure of what they said. To Jack Barley's immense relief, Bannion said, 'Thanks for the water. Let's hit the trail, fellas.'

Jack Barley resumed forking hay until they were over a hill and out of sight. Ellie and Sammy came to the door of the house. 'Stay put!' he ordered them. 'That hill gives them cover to watch from. I'll pitch for another five minutes or so, then I'll come inside.'

At the other side of the hill, Howie Bannion drew rein.

'What're we holdin' up for, Howie?' Dan Bannion questioned. 'There ain't nothin' worth delayin' for.'

'Yeah,' Ike said. 'Let's go rob the bank in Johnson Creek, like we planned.'

'Because,' Howie Bannion replied, 'the sodbuster lied.'

'Lied, Howie?' Ike Bannion quizzed.

' 'Bout what?' Dan Bannion wanted to know.

'The woman,' the outlaw leader said. 'And I've got me a real good idea 'bout robbin' that bank, too.'

Jack Barley had spent the best part of fifteen

minutes forking hay when he finished and walked to the house, figuring that he had allowed enough time for the Bannions to have ridden on, and there was nothing to be gained by hanging round. He was ready for a good laugh with Ellie once he got inside the house. However, as he neared the house, his mood changed dramatically from one of intended banter to one of new trepidation.

The question was, had any of the Bannions seen what he was now looking at?

CHAPTER FOUR

From inside the house, Ellie saw her husband's jaunty step falter. His gaze, which had been directed at the house, had switched to some point beyond the house. Had the men doubled back? Then, in a flash of recall, she knew what had caught Jack's eye. And she also, in the same instant, knew the significance of the female item of washing hanging on the line out back of the house.

Her petticoat!

But was there any cause for alarm? The men had ridden on. However, though she had only had a brief glimpse of the trio's leader, the impression she had gained was of a man who was shrewd and calculating – in fact, the kind of man who missed nothing, sight or sound, mood, too.

Ellie Barley tried desperately to think back. Had the wind blowing now only sprung up? Or had it been blowing while the riders were in the yard? They had ridden in from an angle that would conceal the washline at the rear of the house from view. But the wind that had sprung up would blow the clothes on the line, and from the yard the petticoat might be visible.

Jack Barley let his eyes slide towards the hill over which the Bannions had ridden. He saw no sign of them, but the standing hairs on the back of his neck told him that the trouble he had thought he had avoided had only been postponed.

He continued on to the house, his fears rising. Once inside, he hurried past Ellie and Sammy who were waiting in the hall, to look out the parlour window.

'What's wrong, Pa?' Sammy asked, sensing his parents' tension. 'Are they bad men?'

'Nothing's wrong, Sammy,' he said kindly, to allay the boy's fears, but Sammy was not convinced.

'Maybe they didn't see my petticoat, Jack,' Ellie murmured, joining Barley at the parlour window to look out on the deserted landscape.

Barley looked at her questioningly. It was obvious that she knew the danger that any such sighting would pitch them into.

'A chance in a million,' Barley said, his tone upbeat.

But Ellie Barley's sigh was long and hopeless. 'Sure they did, Jack.'

'It's OK,' Sammy said manfully. 'I'll stand with you, Pa.'

Barley ruffled the youngster's fair hair. 'I never doubted that you wouldn't, partner.' He hugged the boy to him. 'Now why don't you mosey along and help your ma prepare supper. I'll go outside for a look-see.'

Sammy Barley's eyes popped with alarm. 'That could be a pretty dumb move, Pa,' he counselled. 'Those fellas might just be waiting to pick you off.'

'I don't think that's Howie Bannion's way, Sa—'

'Howie Bannion? Crikey! He's the meanest critter ever to walk on earth. And those brothers of his, if a rattler bit them, the rattler would die.'

Barley cursed his stupidity in revealing the identity of the visitors, but he had not expected Sammy's knowledge of the outlaws to be so comprehensive. 'How do you know about the Bannions?' he quizzed.

'Jake Wayne told me.'

'And how does Jake Wayne know about the Bannions?'

'From his uncle Herb. He's a sheriff in New Mexico. Crossed paths with the Bannion brothers a time or two, and was lucky to escape a timber overcoat.'

'Where did you get the colourful lingo? Don't tell me, Jake Wayne?'

'Jake's great, Pa. He's my best friend in school.'

He didn't add that Jake Wayne was his only friend in school. Jake was an independent cuss who made up his own mind who he'd call a friend. One day he'd make a fine man, too.

Ellie Barley had had her reservations about Sammy's friendship with Jake Wayne, as he was from the sort of stock that would worry a parent. But over time, Jack and she had changed their minds about Jake, as he stood squarely with Sammy against those who would mock him because of his limp, and had in fact got a bloody nose a couple of times for the fervency of his protection.

'I guess Jake's cut from a different cloth to his folks,' Ellie had come round to thinking. 'Maybe we should give merit where merit is due, Jack.'

'That's fair, I'd say,' Barley had agreed.

'You ain't really going out there, are you?' Sammy asked, when Barley headed for the door.

'It'll be OK,' Barley reassured Ellie and Sammy.

Outside, storm clouds rolling up from Mexico were painting the landscape black. The wind had lost its freshness, and now the late evening air was thick and cloying. At least the rain would fill the water barrels and replenish the well.

Saddling up, he set out to reconnoitre the surrounding terrain. Beyond the hill over which the Bannion brothers had ridden, the lie of the land lost its farmland flatness to gullies and draws and rock formations that lent themselves to ambush and injury for a careless man. He crested the hill, ready as he could be to deal with any surprises that might be lurking.

He rode and searched for an hour, before he was satisfied that the Bannions had indeed ridden on. He swung round and headed back for home, anticipating supper at his ease.

The storm that had been building finally broke as he drew near the house. Ellie Barley came to the door to wave to him and waited for him to ride up.

'No sign of them,' Barley said. 'I'm starved. What's for supper?'

'Meat pie,' she sang out, her tenseness of feature at odds with the cheeriness in her voice.

Jack Barley was stepping onto the porch when he realized the significance of seeing no lamps lit when he was approaching the house. He had put the lack of lamplight down to Ellie's sparing ways. Coal-oil costs had risen sharply in recent times, and in the precarious financial situation they found themselves, a whole pile of other more urgent commodities had to take precedence over illumination.

However, this time Jack Barley knew that the lack of light was not an economy.

'Howdy, friend.'

Howie Bannion stepped out of the shadows behind Ellie, a hunting knife to Sammy's throat. Dan and Ike Bannion joined him, still chuckling at the idea Howie Bannion had come up with. It was pretty slick thinking. They could have the woman, and the bank loot without risking a single bullet.

CHAPTER FIVE

'Why don't you step in the house, Barley?' Howie Bannion said. 'Wouldn't want you to catch your death from a drenchin'.'

'It's OK, Ellie,' Jack Barley said, sliding an arm round her waist. 'There was nothin' you could do.'

'Nice woman you've got there, Barley,' Dan Bannion sneered.

The youngest of the brothers sidled up to Ellie, rubbing against her like a dog in heat. Barley shoved him away. The force of the push sent the youngest of the brothers sprawling on the floor. Ike Bannion sniggered. Dan Bannion sprang to his feet, his eyes flashing murder.

'Easy, Dan,' Howie Bannion said, stepping between him and Barley. 'A man's got a right and a duty to protect his woman.'

Dan Bannion's anger flared more, until he

saw in his older brother's eyes the startling clear honesty which he could conjure up to hide his black thoughts. In fact the more honesty, the blacker the thoughts. Which meant that right now, with his eyes glowing like those of a saint, Howie Bannion was in the devil's own mood.

'I guess you're right at that, big Brother,' Dan Bannion chuckled, banter replacing angst. A little waiting made a man's eventual pleasure all the keener.

'I think you should apologize to Mrs Barley, Dan,' Howie said.

Dan Bannion's apology was readily forthcoming. 'Sorry, ma'am.'

'Come near my wife again and I'll kill you,' Jack Barley vowed.

'Now, Howie,' Dan complained. 'Ain't that an unfriendly attitude, and me sayin' sorry an' all?'

'Why don't we all step into the kitchen,' Howie Bannion suggested. 'Have some supper and relax.'

'I want you out of my house, right now,' Jack Barley grated, knowing how futile his demand was.

Ike Bannion snarled, 'You keep your trap shut, and listen to what Howie's got to say, mister.'

Again, Howie Bannion acted as peacemaker.

'Now, let's just all settle down here. And no

one'll come to any harm.'

'State what you want, Bannion,' Jack Barley barked.

Howie Bannion glared at Jack Barley. The hand holding the knife to Sammy Barley's throat began to shake. A slight trickle of blood came from the small nick the blade put in the boy's skin, just under his right ear.

Ellie screamed.

'Now look what you've done,' the outlaw whined at Barley. 'Ya see, I get this shake in my hand when folks don't do as I say.'

'Do as he wants, Jack,' Ellie said fretfully. And when her husband did not immediately thaw, added anxiously, 'You don't have a choice!'

'A real sensible woman you've got there, Jack,' Ike Bannion taunted.

Howie Bannion indicated that Barley should walk ahead to the kitchen. 'You keep real still and quiet, boy,' he warned Sammy.

Shocked, Sammy's terrified eyes flashed between his ma and pa.

'Whatever it is you want,' Barley said, addressing Howie Bannion, 'you leave my wife and boy out of it.'

Howie Bannion sat on the edge of the table directly in front of Barley. 'I don't reckon that you're in any position to set terms, Barley,' he growled. Then, relaxing, he added, 'The woman and boy won't be harmed, if you do exactly as I tell you to.'

'And what would that be?'

Howie Bannion rubbed his belly. 'I talk better when I've a full belly.' He turned to Ellie. 'Cook us up some grub, woman.'

Despite the outlaw's firm reassurance, Jack Barley's fears were not set to rest, because there simply was no trusting a man of Howie Bannion's low character.

A couple of miles south of the Barley homestead, a drenched rider cursed the storm that had broken. The deluge had washed away every trace of the men he was tracking – the Bannion brothers.

US Marshal Seth Cleary was in his third week of tracking the outlaws, and had come close a couple of times to nailing them, missing out by only an hour the previous week in a whorehouse down near the border.

He had started out as the leader of a posse from a town called Eagletop where Ike Bannion had killed the mayor, the latest murder in a long line. He had tried to muster a posse, and there were takers before he told them who they were chasing. Within seconds he was alone.

One of the would-be posse summed it up. 'A man might as well put a gun to his head and pull the trigger as hunt down the Bannions, Marshal.'

Cleary agreed wholeheartedly with the gent's summing up. But had still decided that, with the Bannion brothers within a whiff, he'd have to try and hunt them down. Only it hadn't turned out to be that simple. The outlaws were wily and cunning adversaries and they knew the country well, riding trails that a lot of men, including him, did not even know existed.

Eventually, Seth Cleary was faced with the prospect of having to return to Eagletop and admit failure – until earlier that day when he had picked up sign; sign that was now washed away by the damn storm.

'I guess it's true,' he said, eyes clenched against the driving rain and flashing lightning, 'the Devil looks after his own.'

Right up to the minute the storm had broken, he had been following clear sign. Now, sitting astride his horse in the lightning-streaked downpour, he watched the trail turn to mud. He looked out from under the water-laden brim of his Stetson at the terrain ahead and consoled himself that the sign might not be the Bannions anyway.

All he could do was head for the nearest town, a burg called Johnson Creek, he believed. A town of no consequence and no future.

Looking up, he saw a flicker of lamplight. A homestead? The lamplight vanished as quickly as it had shown. But he had the general direction of its location. Of course, if the light did not show again, he could miss the house by miles. Whoever lived there might be of a hospitable frame of mind and give him board.

A sudden fork of lightning lit up the house. Seth Cleary rode on, hoping for a warm fire, hot grub, and a peaceful rest. Tomorrow he'd try and pick up the Bannions' trail again.

CHAPTER SIX

Refreshed, Howie Bannion revealed his scheme and, as he did so, Jack Barley's jaw dropped onto his chest. His response was, 'You must be loco, Bannion!'

Howie Bannion chuckled. 'Some would say,' he said. His chuckle turned to a growl. 'And some who did, ain't able to talk no more.'

'What you ask is impossible, Mr Bannion,' Ellie Barley said.

'*Mr* Bannion,' Dan Bannion laughed. 'You hear that, Ike? *Mr* Bannion, the lady said.'

Ike Bannion's lust-filled eyes were on Ellie. 'I sure do like a polite woman, fellas. Obliging, too, I bet.'

Jack Barley sprang off his chair and reached across the table to grab Ike Bannion. But Howie Bannion shoved him back in his chair.

'Now, don't let's get all het up 'bout nothin',

Barley,' he said. 'Ike didn't mean no harm. You gotta understand that a woman as fine and lovely as your wife will bring out the worst in men.'

He settled back in his chair.

'Now, let's parley 'bout this plan I've got for you to—'

'I'm not going to rob the bank for you, Bannion,' Jack Barley barked. 'And who in tarnation would want to rob the Johnson Creek bank anyway? It's got more spiders in its safe than dollars.'

Howie Bannion let out a long and weary sigh. 'Now that ain't a very friendly attitude, is it?'

'It's the only attitude you're going to get!'

The outlaw leader slid a glance Ike Bannion's way, which was immediately understood. Ike leapt out of his chair and grabbed Ellie round the waist, pressing himself against her, moaning. Ellie's face twisted in disgust as his thick, oily lips slid along her throat.

'You leave my ma alone!' Sammy yelled, kicking out at Ike Bannion with his good leg, catching the outlaw right on the kneecap.

Ike Bannion swung at the boy, lifting him off his feet with a side-swipe that pitched him across the room. Howie Bannion's sixgun flashed from its holster to dissuade Barley from any rashness.

'Please, Jack,' Ellie pleaded. 'Don't make things worse than they are.'

'Let the woman go, Ike,' Howie instructed his brother.

'Heck, Howie,' he groused. 'And me just gettin' all warmed up.'

'Let her be!'

Ike Bannion raised his hands. 'OK, big Brother. Don't twist a gut.'

Ellie hurried to pick up Sammy from the corner where he sat dazed.

'Don't fuss. I'm OK, Ma. They don't scare me none.'

'Let the boy go to his room,' she pleaded with Howie Bannion. 'He's got no part in this.'

'You promise to behave, boy?' Bannion asked.

'Of course he will,' Ellie answered. 'Won't you, Sammy? For me and your pa.'

'Sure I will, Ma,' he said dejectedly.

'I'll tuck you in.'

Dan Bannion volunteered, 'I'll go help, ma'am.'

Dan Bannion went to escort Ellie into the bedroom.

'Now, don't you get up to nothin' naughty, Dan,' Ike Bannion sneered.

Howie Bannion's flinty eyes held a clearly understood message for Jack Barley.

The anger boiled inside Barley; anger that was driven by his helplessness to protect his family. He could see the disappointment in Sammy's eyes, whose young mind could not grasp why his father was seemingly so cowardly. And the decision he'd reached would only be seen by Sammy as further evidence of his cowardice.

'I'll rob the bank for you, Bannion,' he told Howie.

Howie Bannion's smile was one of pure triumph. 'A very sensible and wise decision, Barley.' He addressed Dan Bannion, 'Sit, Dan.'

Primed to have fun, the youngest of the outlaws did not take kindly to being reined in. Ike Bannion's snide snigger did not help.

'I guess you're going to have to cool all that hot blood flowing in your veins, little Brother,' he taunted.

'Shut your trap, Ike,' Howie Bannion snarled.

Ike Bannion's face became ugly. 'You're dishin' out a whole pile of orders, Howie.'

'That's 'cause I'm the boss of this outfit, Ike,' Howie said. 'And if you don't like it,' he nodded, 'the door's open.'

'You'd kick me out?'

Howie Bannion's hard face was uncompromising.

Dan Bannion stepped in. 'As he says, Ike. Howie's the boss.'

Ike Bannion was out of options and out of allies. He laughed harshly. 'Yeah, I guess that's the way it's always been.'

'And always will be,' Howie reminded the middle brother of the three.

Ike Bannion said nothing. But what he was thinking was right there in his narrowed eyes. It would not be long before Ike challenged his brother for the leadership of the outfit.

'How am I suppose to rob the bank?' Jack Barley asked.

For a split-second, Marshal Seth Cleary saw the flicker of light again and changed direction towards its source. It was hard to tell, but he reckoned that the light was not far away. A lamp in a homestead window, he guessed. A beam of hope to a lost traveller.

'Hope they're friendly folk,' he murmured. 'Just what I need.'

And maybe the folk in the house had seen three riders go by, and could tell him which way they were headed.

CHAPTER SEVEN

'The bank is about to call in your loan.'

'How the hell do you know that?' Barley challenged Howie Bannion.

'It's common knowledge round these parts. Dan drifted into town a couple days ago, stopped by the saloon. Liquor loosens tongues. If you want to know how a town ticks, who's who and what's what, a saloon's the place to find out.

'Dan overheard talk 'bout your difficulties. Seems you ain't the most pop'lar man in these parts. Talk was that you deserve what's comin' down the line, 'cause you shirked your duty to fight in the war.

'No man likes a fella who hid under the bed when other men were dyin'.'

Coming from the bedroom after settling Sammy down, Ellie Barley put forward a spirited defence of her husband's stance in the conflict between North and South.

'There's other ways to resolve differences other than shot and shell. If you ask me, this country could do with a lot more talking and a lot less shooting, Mr Bannion!'

Howie Bannion ignored Ellie's outburst, and went on, 'You've got fields of rotten crops 'cause no one is buyin' from you, Barley. Now the way I figure, you're in a dead end alley. Sell up, and you'll not get anyway near a fair price. Stay put, and the bank will foreclose. Either way you end up penniless.'

Howie Bannion paused to let the sense of his argument settle. But Bannion was telling him nothing new. Jack Barley had been tussling with his dilemma for months now, and no matter how much thought he gave his predicament, a solution to it seemed even more impossible to find by the day.

'You're goin' to have to clear outa this country, Barley. Mexico, maybe. South of the border they don't give a hoot what uniform, if any, a man wore. If you've got dinero, Mexes don't give a shit.'

'I don't have money,' Barley said. 'If I had I wouldn't have a problem to begin with.'

Howie Bannion's shrewd eyes glistened.

'You could have,' he said temptingly. 'My brothers and me would cut you in for a share of the bank loot.' He glanced at Ike and Dan Bannion. 'Ain't that so, fellas?'

'Sure is,' Ike said.

'I'm no thief,' Barley stated sternly. 'In my book a man's only got a right to what he's earned.'

Howie Bannion pushed back his hat and scratched his head. 'Mighty principled words, Barley. But your wife and boy can't eat principles.' He leaned forward towards Barley. 'How long d'ya think it'll be before their bellies are hollow?'

On seeing how cleverly Bannion had raised the spectre that had haunted her husband, Ellie Barley urged, 'Don't listen to him, Jack. It's the Devil talking in the guise of Howie Bannion.'

'Devil or not,' the outlaw leader said, 'I'm talkin' sense, ma'am. And you know I am, Barley.'

'And how am I suppose to rob the bank?' Barley asked resignedly.

'Jack,' Ellie pleaded. 'Don't listen.'

'Bannion is making sense, Ellie,' he flung back. 'We're only hanging on by a thread here. The bank will have the shirt off my back in weeks.'

He turned his attention back to Howie Bannion.

'You didn't answer my question.'

'Simple, like all the best plans are.' He settled to explaining the way a man would with a *compadre.* 'You'll ride into town tonight—'

'Tonight?' Barley exclaimed. 'Banks are closed at night.'

Dan Bannion cut loose with a hyena laugh. 'That's the best time to rob 'em.'

Howie Bannion continued with the elaboration of his plan. 'You'll call on the bank president—'

'You just don't drop by Charles Archer's house. At least not when you haven't got two dimes to rub together.'

Howie Bannion nodded to his brother Ike, who slung the bulging saddle-bag he'd been keeper of across the table. The outlaw leader opened the saddle-bag and took from it a bound packet of one hundred dollar bills.

'A little something we relieved the railroad of a week ago,' he chuckled. He shoved the bills across the table to Jack Barley. 'Real pretty, ain't they?' he tempted. 'Go on, Barley. Pick 'em up.'

'Leave them be, Jack,' Ellie pleaded.

'Be quiet, woman!'

Ellie was stung by her husband's sharp-tongued rebuke. In their ten years of marriage, it was the first time he had spoken to her with such venom. Tears flooded her eyes.

'No caterwauling,' Barley added, even more

harshly. 'I think it would be best if you left Howie and me to work out the details of this bank robbery in private, Ellie.'

Astonished, Ellie Barley stood rooted to the spot. She watched, as if hypnotized, as her husband picked up a packet of dollar bills and considered it greedily.

'Git, woman!' he barked.

Crying, Ellie fled the room.

Ike Bannion stood up. 'Maybe I should go and comfort the lady.'

'She'll be fine,' Barley growled.

Howie Bannion shot his brother a snake-eyed look. He had Barley on the hook, and all he needed was another couple of smooth-talking minutes to land him. Ike Bannion, his face greasy with the sweat of lust, very reluctantly held back.

'Feel nice, don't they?' Howie Bannion purred, reaching out to press Jack Barley's hand over the bills. 'Now I'm goin' to give you two thousand dollars to tempt Archer from his fireside.

'You tell him that you've sold up and want to settle accounts. Tell him that you don't want to keep all this money in the house overnight. That'll make sense. That you want it safe and sound in the bank, so that your last night in these parts will be a restful one.'

'Archer will never believe that I've got a buyer,' Barley said. 'Selling this place would be like selling sand in the damn desert.'

Howie Bannion shook his head. 'Archer will be a banker lookin' at a whole pile of cash that he'll want to get his greedy hands on. Tomorrow will be soon enough to ponder on the miracle of anyone loco enough to buy your farm.'

'He'll want to know who the buyer is,' Barley cautioned.

'Tell him that's a secret the new owner wants to keep until he's ready to show his hand.'

After pondering for a spell, Jack Barley said, 'Archer's a greedy bastard, sure enough. This scheme of yours could very well work, Howie.'

'I know it will,' the outlaw leader boasted.

Howie Bannion began to laugh, and his laughter grew until it filled every inch of the house. His brothers joined in. Then Bannion's laughter finished as quickly as it had begun.

'One thing, Barley,' he said, beady-eyed. 'Don't you go gettin' no ideas 'bout stuffin' your pockets and skippin' the bank robbery. Or, for that matter, hightailin' it after heistin' the bank. I reckon it's 'bout a two-hour round trip to town and back. Allowin' for, say, fifteen minutes for Archer to reach the bank and the robbery done, I'll be expectin' you back in no later than two and a half. And if you're not . . . well, you just keep thinkin' of your wife and boy.'

'And you keep in mind that if Ellie and Sammy are harmed, I'll kill you, somehow,' Barley said.

Howie Bannion studied Barley. 'I think you might try at that. Have we got ourselves a deal?'

Jack Barley nodded.

The neighing of a horse had the outlaws on guard.

'Are you expectin' company?' Howie Bannion urgently enquired of Barley.

'No one ever visits. I'm an outcast, remember?'

Ike Bannion had crossed to the window and was peeping out the side of the curtain. 'A lone rider,' he said.

'The loft,' Barley said.

He hurried from the kitchen, the outlaws on his tail. He grabbed a ladder standing against the wall and placed it against the opening to the loft. Howie and Ike Bannion climbed into the loft, but Dan Bannion held back, sweating and breathing hard.

'Come on, Dan,' Howie Bannion ordered. 'Git up here!'

'Ya know how I hate tight spaces, Howie,' he griped. 'Can't breathe proper in them.'

'Prefer a bullet in the gut from Cleary?' Howie snarled.

Shaking, Dan Bannion climbed into the loft.

'No tricks, Barley,' Howie Bannion warned.

Jack Barley closed the hatch and climbed back down. He placed the ladder against the wall. 'Everything must appear to be perfectly normal, Ellie.'

'Normal,' she scoffed. 'Nothing will ever be normal again, Jack. Now that you've taken up with new friends.'

The coldness of her tone stung him, but he understood the reason for her frostiness. She was seeing a new Jack Barley. A man she did not like. Couldn't she understand that he had to play along with the Bannions to keep her and Sammy safe? He was not fooled for a second by Howie Bannion's bonhomie. Besides the loot from the bank, there was another prize to be taken; a prize that would be taken there and then if he refused to do as the outlaws wanted – Ellie herself. Appearing to co-operate with the Bannions bought him time. What he could do with that time, if anything, he did not yet know.

'Hello, the house,' a man called out.

'Like I said, Ellie,' Barley cautioned. 'Everything must appear as normal.'

Jack Barley went to the door to answer the visitor's summons.

'A hellish night,' the rider greeted him.

'That it surely is,' Barley said conversationally.

'Seth Cleary's the name,' the man said, dismounting.

'Jack Barley.'

He stepped aside to let the drenched man enter.

'Ma'am,' he greeted Ellie. And picking up on her tension, added, 'I surely hope that I'm not imposing at an inopportune time?'

Ellie smiled. 'No. Not at all. Mr Cleary, isn't it?'

'Yes, ma'am. Marshal Seth Cleary.'

In the loft, on hearing the name, the Bannion brothers shot each other alarmed looks. Cleary had been tracking them, relentless and dogged in his pursuit. They had had droves of lawmen dogging their tails, but of them all Seth Cleary was the one they feared most. The outlaws saw it as their misfortune that he happened to be in Eagletop when they had robbed the bank. With the help of the storm, they had shaken him off.

Now he was right back on their doorstep!

CHAPTER EIGHT

'What'll we do, Howie?' Dan Bannion fretted in a hoarse whisper, shifting uneasily and gasping, his eyes wild with panic.

'Kill the bastard, of course,' was Ike Bannion's solution to their problem.

Howie Bannion was frowning, the appearance of Seth Cleary was a problem which he had not planned for.

'Well?' Ike pressed his older brother.

'We sit tight,' the outlaw leader decided.

'And what'll that do for us?' Ike demanded to know.

'Yeah, Howie,' Dan Bannion pitched in. 'Cleary'll probably bed down for the night.' His eyes grew wilder still as he took in the dark and claustrophobic confines of the loft.

'And that means that Barley won't be able to rob the damn bank for us,' Ike Bannion put in.

'You've got to think of somethin', Howie,' Dan urged. He ran his finger round the collar of his shirt. 'I can't breathe in this rat's hole.'

'How am I suppose to think if you fellas keep grousin' all the time!' Howie said, tight-lipped.

'Why don't you come through to the kitchen, Mr Cleary?' Ellie invited.

'That'll be Seth, ma'am.'

'I've got some left over meat pie, Seth.'

'Mightily obliged, folks,' Cleary drawled.

In the loft, Ike Bannion, who was nearest to the opening, said, 'All I've got to do is lift this panel and blast him as he passes along the hall, Howie.'

'Wait!' Howie Bannion commanded.

'For what, Howie?' Dan Bannion asked nervously.

'I don't know. But Barley will be aware of us sittin' on top of him, and what it'll mean if he don't do as I said. So I figure that he'll find some way to get rid of Cleary.'

'You'd better be figurin' right, big Brother,' Ike said, a threat in his tone.

Howie Bannion let the threat go unchallenged. But he knew that at a time not too far off, he'd have to restake his claim to the leadership of the outfit because of Ike's ambition to be top dog. And Dan Bannion knew that soon he would have to choose between his brothers. Or maybe he'd take his share of the bank robbery loot and vamoose across the border. That was, of course, if he did not choke to death in the cramped and dusty loft. And, also, provided that his rising panic did not make him loco enough to leap from it. His claustrophobia came from being locked in the woodshed as a boy for two days as a punishment by his pa with not a crack of light showing. If Pa had any use at all, it was as a carpenter. But he was mostly too drunk to use a saw and retain his arm.

Howie Bannion looked at the sheen of sweat on his kid brother's face and at the wild panic showing in his eyes and knew that the bomb ticking inside Dan Bannion could explode at any second. Dan Bannion shifted uneasy legs and, in the hall below, a wisp of dust drifted past Seth Cleary's face. Barley recognized the danger of that wisp of dust. Would Cleary? Apparently oblivious to what the dust might mean, the marshal followed Ellie into the kitchen.

Sammy, curious about their visitor, came from his room to the kitchen just as Seth Cleary was removing his rawhide jacket to reveal a US marshal's badge.

'Howdy, young feller,' Cleary greeted Sammy.

Sammy Barley's eyes lit up with hope on discovering that their visitor was a lawman, anticipating a problem solved.

'Howdy, sir,' Sammy greeted respectfully.

'A fine boy,' Cleary complimented Ellie.

Fearing an outburst from Sammy, Jack Barley said sternly, 'Now that you've met our guest, Sammy, best go right back to bed.'

Also conscious of the danger that Sammy would attempt to make Cleary aware of the outlaws holed up in the loft, Ellie hurried to remove Sammy from the marshal's presence.

'But, Ma,' he protested, his gaze firmly on Seth Cleary.

'You want to say something, son?' the lawman asked.

In the loft, the Bannion Brothers tensed, their hands instinctively dropping to their guns.

'You mustn't bother the marshal, Sammy,' Ellie said, sweeping him along with her out of the kitchen. The Bannions' relaxed, but not much.

'That young feller really wanted to gab, didn't he?' Cleary said curiously.

'We don't get much company,' Barley said by way of explanation to cover Sammy's eagerness to talk.

Cleary rubbed his chin, his expression thoughtful. 'Seemed to get real excited when he saw the marshal's badge.'

'A boy of that age is impressionable. A head full of town-taming lawmen and fast guns.'

Ellie came back into the kitchen. 'I'll serve up that meat pie now, Marshal.'

In the loft, Howie Bannion was more tense than he could ever remember being before. From what he heard of the conversation in the house below, it was looking like the hound-dog marshal was getting ready to stay around for a longish spell.

'How do we know Barley ain't scribblin' a message on a piece of paper right now, Howie?' Ike Bannion said, setting new fires of panic in Dan.

'Ike could be right, Howie,' the youngest of the brothers said croakily. 'Let's kill the badge-toter. I'm damn well smotherin' in this rat-trap.'

'The storm is passing. He'll be on his way in no time at all,' Howie falsely opined.

'I figure Cleary is countin' on being an over-nighter, Howie,' Ike said.

'Barley knows he's got to get rid of Cleary. And I reckon he will.'

'Haven't tasted pie as good as this for a heck of a long time, ma'am,' Seth Cleary complimented Ellie Barley. 'And I was wondering if I might impose on your hospitality 'til morning.'

'Well. . . .'

'If I was familiar with the country I'd head for the nearest town and not be a bother,' Cleary said, to overcome Ellie Barley's hesitancy.

'You can ride in with me, Marshal.'

The Bannion brothers ears pricked up and they exchanged alarmed glances.

'What game's he playin' at, Howie?' Dan Bannion wondered, his whisper beginning to rise.

Howie Bannion slapped a hand over Dan's mouth. 'Want Cleary to hear us?' he growled.

'Don't want to be a bother,' Cleary said. 'If you don't want me in the house, I can bunk down in the barn.'

'No bother,' Jack Barley said. 'You finish that pie and we'll start for town.'

'I guess I'll leave it,' the marshal said, his tone brusque. The Bannions could hear the scrape of Cleary's plate on the rough wooden table as he pushed it away from him. 'I've obviously worn out my welcome.'

'He's ridin' to town to rob the bank with a lawman in tow!' Ike Bannion said in disbelief.

'As soon as he's out of the house, he'll tell that bastard marshal 'bout us, Howie,' Dan fretted.

'Prob'ly come ridin' back with a posse,' Ike added.

But Howie Bannion was shaking his head. 'Barley will keep his trap shut and do as we want, 'cause of the woman and the boy.' The outlaw relaxed. 'They're what makes life worth livin' for him.'

'I sure hope you're callin' this right, Howie,' Ike Bannion said darkly.

'And if I'm not, Brother?' Howie said, picking up on the unspoken threat in Ike's prickly statement.

Ike Bannion's scowling stare clashed with Howie's challenging gaze, and suddenly the loft bristled with tension.

'Howie's always been right, Ike,' Dan Bannion said, pouring oil on troubled waters.

On shifting ground, Ike Bannion dropped his scowling appearance. 'Sure he has, Dan,' he said, in the charming way he could when the T in trouble was too big for him. 'I guess I'm worryin' 'bout nothin'.'

'I can offer you a fresh horse,' Jack Barley offered the marshal.

'I guess mine's got enough grit left to make town,' Seth Cleary said in a clipped tone of voice. 'So let's get going.' Then, 'By the way, did you folk see three riders in these parts?'

Barley shook his head. 'Can't say I have, Marshal.'

'You, ma'am?'

'No, Marshal,' Ellie answered confidently.

Cleary led the way out of the kitchen and the house.

When they heard the sound of riders departing, Ike Bannion said, 'Time to have us some fun and games with the woman, fellas.'

'After Barley returns with the money,' Howie said.

'Why wait?' Ike challenged.

'If Barley returns to find that his woman's been harmed, he'll charge us like a loco bull.'

'Then we'll shoot him,' was Dan Bannion's simple remedy.

'We might not stop him before he rips one of our heads off,' Howie said, and stated finally, 'Loot first. We kill Barley. Then we take the woman.'

'That's a real good plan, Howie,' Dan Bannion agreed.

Ike Bannion grinned lewdly, his thoughts obviously racing ahead to the pleasures to come.

CHAPTER NINE

'Point the way, mister,' Seth Cleary said sourly, when they were a short distance from the house. 'I have no wish to share the trail with a man who doesn't want my company.'

'I never said that I didn't want your company, Marshal,' Jack Barley snapped.

'Sure looked like that to me, fella.'

'It's just that room is tight at the house.'

'You had a barn,' Cleary flung back.

'It leaks all over.'

The lawman scoffed and looked to the sky from which rain was pouring down. 'Not as much as this damn roof!'

Jack Barley gave him no argument on that fact.

'There's only one trail to town that's any way safe in this storm,' he said. 'There's a couple of canyon trails that are shorter, but a man would be risking flash floods in those now. And it makes no sense to me that we shouldn't share the trail, seeing that there's only one.'

They rode on in silence for a spell before Cleary spoke. 'If you don't mind my saying so, Barley, you seem to be carrying a weight on your shoulders that's threatening to break your back.'

Barley shrugged. 'Sodbusting isn't easy. It's a sun-up to sun-down struggle to make ends meet.'

'Then why do you do it?' Cleary asked bluntly.

'It's what I know.'

'You could learn new tricks, couldn't you?'

'I'm forty-two years old, Marshal. New tricks aren't learned easily.'

'I used to punch cows,' Seth Cleary said, as if he was confessing a cardinal sin. 'Hated the smelly critters. So one day, while on a trail drive, I came across a hick town called Wiley Junction – the junction had been in the expectation that a rail spur would come the town's way – it didn't. It was the kind of place that if one building collapsed the rest would too, because they were leaning on each other for support.

'On my way to the saloon, I saw a notice on the law-office bulletin board. The town was looking for a part-time sheriff. Mostly to run drunks in on a Saturday night. Paid in kind. A clapboard house and free grub. A couple of dollars thrown in for baccy and beer. The notice was mighty dusty and tattered, like it had been pinned to the board for a heck of a long time. So I figured that the town would hand the sheriff's badge to any man who was fool enough to pin it on.'

He chuckled in a musical baritone voice.

'Spent a whole hour trying to persuade the mayor that I wasn't joshing him. When I finally convinced him that he had a candidate for the job, he had a badge on me faster than a rattler's fang.

'A week later, I got a hellfire baptism. A fella by the name of Sam Dewey rode in, on the very same day that a dodger for him landed on my desk. He was wanted for bank robbery and murder and most other things too.

'I took no pride in skulking in the sheriff's office, but I wasn't gun-slick back then. Shit, the only use I'd made of a shooter up to that time was as a makeshift hammer for putting to rights any stray nails on fence posts and the like.

'I soon found out that Sam Dewey was the kind of man who liked to shove a man's face deeper into the dirt than it already was. Second day in town, he called me out.'

His attention gripped by Seth Cleary's story, which he was relating with the gift of an ace story-teller, Jack Barley asked, 'How come you're still sucking air?'

'Luck,' Cleary stated. 'Dewey liked to sling his sixgun low. When he drew on me, the hammer of the Colt snagged on a rip in the leg of his trousers. When I shot him, his .45 slid back into its holster and the story got around that I was so darn fast that Sam Dewey's gun never cleared leather.

'That story spread like a damn bushfire. So, I figured sensibly, that fellas looking to build a rep would come looking to find the man who had out-gunned Sam Dewey. And before that happened, I had the good sense to hightail it out of Wiley Junction.

'By now I'd taken a shine to wearing a badge. Figured that I wouldn't mind toting one long term. So I spent the next couple of months learning to handle a sixgun, and any other gun I got my hands on.'

He drew rein.

'And the point is, Barley, that a man doesn't have to do what he's always done. If you look hard enough, there's always another way out of your troubles.'

'Who said anything about troubles?' Barley said, a mite too quickly.

Seth Cleary said bluntly, 'Your crops are rotting in the fields, Barley. Repairs are going undone. And your woman, though fighting bravely, is close to being beaten. You've got troubles sure enough. And the problem with troubles is that they don't get any smaller by pretending you don't have them.'

Jack Barley laughed, but his laughter soon lost its cavalier nature.

'They looked like good crops,' Cleary said. 'Crops that should have found a ready buyer. Can't help wonder why they didn't?'

'It seems that around here crops are only as good as the man who grows them,' Jack Barley said grimly.

'Which means, I guess, that you're a Reb in Yankee country?'

'Neither Reb nor Yankee,' Barley said, for the first time ashamed of his pacifist stance in the war. Cleary kindly waited for an explanation before condemning. Which, in Jack Barley's book, marked him out as a fair-minded man. 'I've got beliefs that don't accommodate war, Mr Cleary.'

'You never stood a chance of selling a single crop. In fact, if you were growing stalks of pure gold, I doubt if in this bitter post-war climate that anyone would want them.

'Now if you had been a Yankee, or a Reb, you could have moved to where the colour suited. But having no colour at all makes you an outcast wherever you put down roots.'

Seth Cleary had unequivocally stated the case.

'Mexico, maybe,' he concluded.

Jack Barley became thoughtful. 'Maybe,' he said.

Seth Cleary pulled off the trail to take shelter under a tree to roll a smoke. He proffered the tobacco to Barley.

'Thanks. Don't smoke.'

'Heck, ain't you got any vices at all, mister?'

'I live my life by what it says in the Good Book, Marshal.'

'Never read anything in the Bible about a man not taking a drag of the weed,' Seth Cleary observed. He snorted. 'Not that I'd claim familiarity with the sacred text.'

Cleary fired up the smoke.

'You're not a religious man, then?' Jack Barley asked.

'I talk,' he pointed skywards, 'when talking's needed. And that's usually when the odds are stacked against me and I want to hedge my bets. When the odds are evened out, I don't bother the Good Lord again until there's more talking to be done.'

'Seems disrespectful to me,' Barley stated.

'Can't say that I disagree with you, Barley. But I met an old-timer once who said that there are many pathways to Heaven and each man has to choose his own.' He chuckled. 'And if you bother God every day, ain't there a chance that

He'll get plumb tired of your caterwauling?'

Despite his shock at Seth Cleary's over-casual view of God, the lawman's infectious laughter had Jack Barley laughing along with him. When their mirth subsided, Cleary studied Barley closely.

'Kinda late for a family man to be going to town, ain't it?'

Jack Barley became suddenly and acutely conscious of the stacks of dollar bills tucked inside his shirt. What if he came clean with Cleary and told him about the Bannions lurking in his attic? He had been mighty tempted to do so when they were back at the house, but had decided that any disclosure would see the lawman dead before he got time to draw his next breath. And there was the risk of the Bannions blasting through the ceiling, and he was haunted by the terrible peril that such an outcome would bring to Ellie and Sammy.

So what if he told Cleary now? There were two of them. But they were outside and the Bannions inside the house, with Ellie and Sammy at their mercy. Their safe delivery from danger had to be his first and only concern. And the only way he could ensure their safety was by doing exactly as Howie Bannion had asked.

Beyond that was an imponderable.

'Business,' he replied, in answer to Seth

Cleary's question.

'At this time of night?'

'Do you always ask so many questions?' Barley barked.

'I'm a lawman. Asking questions is second nature to me. That's all I do most days.'

'Ever take a day off? Like now.'

'Touchy kinda *hombre,* ain't ya.' He flicked his smoke into the air. 'Best get this journey over and see the back of each other as soon as we can, I reckon.'

The last couple of miles to town were spent in silence, which was broken by Seth Cleary at the edge of town. Unimpressed by what he saw, the marshal enquired, obviously not hopeful of a positive answer, 'Has this burg got a hotel or a good boarding-house?'

'No hotel. One boarding-house,' Jack Barely pointed. 'The last house at the end of the main street.'

'Clean?'

Barley shrugged.

Seth Cleary glowered at Barley. 'Those riders I was asking about—'

'Told you, Marshal. Didn't see any riders.'

' 'Night, Barley.'

Seth Cleary rode on.

Jack Barley waited until Cleary was lost in the downpour, before turning back out of town to retrace his steps to the bank president's house located a little way south of town, away from the common rabble. Bank presidents could afford exclusivity.

He hitched his horse to a tree at the side of it, out of view of any curious passers-by. It was unlikely that there would be anyone about on the raw night it was. But, being a cautious man, Jack Barley saw no point in taking even the minimal risk involved. Someone might get curious and come calling.

As he made his way to the front door, Barley forced himself not to think beyond the immediate couple of minutes he was facing into. He dared not think about what he'd do when and if he successfully robbed the bank.

'Living witnesses can put a man's neck in a noose.'

Howie Bannion's words echoed in his head, as he hammered on the front door with the fancy brass knocker.

Charles Archer's huge shadow loomed up on the glass panels of the door. He was a man who ate well and often. The front door was yanked open. The bank president's surprise was total.

'Barley. What are you doing here? And on a night that's not fit to be out in, too.'

'Howdy, Mr Archer,' Barley greeted the

banker affably. 'I've come to clear my debt to the bank.'

Archer's surprise turned to astonishment. 'And how do you aim to do that?'

'I found a buyer for the farm.'

'Well, I'll be!'

'I've got the money right here.' Jack Barley opened a couple of buttons on his shirt to reveal the packets of $100 dollar bills. Archer's eyes lit up. His greed was palpable. 'Didn't want to keep all this cash in the house overnight you understand, sir.'

'Of course. That would have been most unwise.'

'I know that my dropping by now is mighty inconvenient. But if you could come along to the bank and—'

'No need for that,' the bank president said. 'If you step into the parlour, I'll give you a note and you can drop by the bank tomorrow during normal business hours to get an official receipt.'

Barley had not expected this turn of events, but he recovered well.

'Well, half of this money is Ellie's. And she'd not sleep well if I didn't bring back an official receipt, Mr Archer.'

'Are you questioning my honesty, Barley?' the banker growled.

'No, sir. But you'll understand how difficult a

fretting woman can make a man's life. And besides, I aim to be out of here first light. The new owner wants to take immediate possession.'

'Who is this new owner?'

'Well, he says that folk will know soon enough without me blabbing it out. Made me take an oath not to reveal his name.'

When Archer hesitated, Jack Barley fiddled with his shirt buttons to give the banker another glimpse of the packets of dollar bills.

'Well,' he said, licking his fat lips, 'wouldn't want Ellie's sleep disturbed.' He grabbed his coat from the hallstand.

'Much obliged,' Barley said.

'Most irregular, of course. Opening up the bank at this hour.'

'We won't need much light. The more light the more curiosity.'

As they walked along the main street to the bank, Jack Barley was glad of the storm's downpour, but would have preferred the absence of the lightning that every now and then trapped him and the bank president in its brilliant light. The lightning's exposure lasted only seconds, but they were seconds that Barley lived through in dread of being seen by some stray night owl.

The town had come into existence on the promise that an ore find held out. But the quality of the ore quickly deteriorated and became difficult to sell and the mine folded. Some upped roots and moved on. However, as always, some men who had suffered one disappointment too many hadn't got the gumption to seek new pastures and became down-and-outs, bumming grub and liquor and sleeping in the backlots or buildings which had fallen into disrepair. And the immediate danger to him was the risk of crossing paths with one of those down-and-outs.

Johnson Creek was a town on its last legs.

Not for the first time since Howie Bannion had proposed robbing the bank, Jack Barley wondered why he'd want to. As banks went, the Johnson Creek bank was a peanuts bank. The whole operation was run by Archer and a part-time teller. No sooner had he begun pondering on the *why*, the bank president put an end to his speculation.

'We've got to be careful, Barley,' Charles Archer confided in a whispered aside. 'The bank safe has fifty thousand dollars in it tonight.'

'Fif—' Jack Barley's jaw dropped.

'Ever hear of Julius H. Ponderfoot?'

Barley shook his head. 'That's a name I'd remember.'

'Well, it's rumoured that Ponderfoot's got more gold than the United States mint,' the banker elaborated, and further explained, 'Letitia Ponderfoot,

Julius's wife, was on a visit to Mexico a couple of months ago. Passed through a village called El Cobra. Just outside the village bandits attempted to kidnap her for ransom, but the villagers fought them off. As a gesture of thanks and goodwill, she convinced her husband to make a donation to the village – a donation of fifty thousand dollars.'

'But how has the money ended up in your bank?' Barley wanted to know.

'Simple.' An intense flash of lightning lit up the street, highlighting the shabby thoroughfare. 'Who'd expect the bank in this one-horse burg to have fifty thousand in its safe.'

How about a fella called Howie Bannion? Jack Barley thought. Obviously Ponderfoot's security was not all that it should be. Someone had squealed to Howie Bannion. Now, at least, he needn't wonder anymore.

Archer leaned closer.

'The money was delivered to the bank under the guise of a shipment of bank stationery.' He chuckled. 'Imagine, Barley. Fifty thousand inside a plain wooden box. My heart near stopped when I opened the box and saw it. There was a note attached, penned by Julius H. Ponderfoot himself, explaining the circumstances and reason for the unusual assignment. I was to simply put the money in the safe, close up and go home. That way attention would not be drawn to the bank, he said.

'Tomorrow, three men, all former US marshals, will call to the bank. They'll have a password that's been given to them directly by Julius Ponderfoot, which I, of course, know. They'll collect and convey the money to the Mexican village, where Ponderfoot appointees will manage and disperse the funds.

'For my pains, I'll be given a fee of five thousand,' he said, breathlessly.

'Haven't you taken a risk telling me this, Mr Archer?' Barley said.

'Risk? Heck, no. You're Jack Barley. You live your life by the Good Book.'

There was a time when he would have been immensely pleased by such a compliment. However, his life of sober propriety and good living had left him way behind in the prosperity stakes, compared to men who had only used the Bible as a prop to steady a chair or table leg. That, to Barley, was beginning to seem mighty unfair and unjust.

$50,000.

The sum kept echoing inside his head, making him dizzy. And the more it echoed, the more Barley's resolve to not make the money his own, slipped. The Devil was tugging at his tail, nibbling away at the upright man Jack Barley was – but might not be for much longer.

CHAPTER TEN

When Jack Barley left, Ike Bannion was the first of the Bannion trio to drop down from the loft. 'You sure look a picture in that gingham gown, ma'am,' he said, his voice as raspy as the scrape of a rusty nail on stone.

'A real temptation, Ike,' Dan Bannion said, dropping down from the loft after his older brother, his eyes fixed lustfully on Ellie Barley.

Ellie backed away from Ike Bannion, her heart leaping into her mouth. The breath in her lungs vanished and she felt weak. Dan Bannion drew level with Ike and tried to edge in front, but Ike Bannion was having none of it and pushed him roughly aside.

'There was no call to do that, Ike,' the youngest of the brothers complained sourly, massaging his left shoulder where it had collided with the edge of the parlour door.

'I wouldn't have, if you had manners,' Ike flung back acrimoniously. 'Can't you see that this fine lady is not used to rough-house antics.'

Howie Bannion quickly stepped between his brothers.

'Settle down,' he ordered.

Ellie went to squeeze past Ike Bannion, who stepped forward to narrow further the already tight space, forcing her to brush against him. His grin was one of pure hellish evil. Howie Bannion grabbed Ike and shoved him aside.

'Sorry, ma'am,' he apologized to Ellie.

Despite Howie Bannion's black-hearted reputation, Ellie reckoned that his apology was genuine, which surprised her. Ellie fled into Sammy's room and shut the door.

'That bitch has locked us out, Howie!' Dan Bannion snarled. 'Well, I ain't standin' for it!'

Howie Bannion checked Dan's charge to the bedroom door.

'Hey, you ain't plannin' on keepin' the woman all for yourself are ya, big Brother?' Ike Bannion asked meanly.

'Leave the woman be,' the outlaw leader grated. 'Business before pleasure.'

Dan and Ike Bannion exchanged suspicious looks.

'I guess we can wait a spell longer, little Brother,' Ike told Dan Bannion.

*

They were past the saloon, which Jack Barley saw as the main risk in being discovered, and were close to the bank when Seth Cleary loomed up in a flash of lightning.

'Howdy, gents,' he greeted Barley and Archer.

Not used to having his path blocked by any man, Charles Archer pompously reprimanded the marshal. 'You're blocking my way, sir.'

Seth Cleary was unperturbed by the banker's starchy protest. His gaze fixed on Jack Barley. 'Where are you fellas headed?'

'Inquisitive sort, aren't you?' Archer stated, his mood soured further by Cleary's out-of-hand dismissal of his protest. 'Our business is none of yours, sir.'

Archer pushed past the marshal, Jack Barley on his coat tails.

'Late for bank business, ain't it?'

Archer came up short, alarmed. 'What makes you think—?'

'Duds,' Seth Cleary interjected. 'Two things you can be, mister: a banker, or an undertaker. Now add those fine jowls to the duds and it has to be a banker, I reckon. And Barley told me that he was coming to town on business.

'It doesn't take the brightest wick to figure it out.'

The blood was draining from Charles Archer's face, and understandably so, Barley thought. With $50,000 in the bank safe, the last thing he'd want was the attentions of a stranger to town. Fearing that Archer would rethink his visit to the bank, Barley hastily stepped in.

'You're a quick-witted fella, Marshal,' he said with a chuckle.

'Marshal?' The banker relaxed visibly.

'Shucks, you gents will have to excuse my bad manners,' Jack Barley said in self-rebuke. 'Mr Archer, this fine cut of a fella is US Marshal Seth Cleary.'

Relaxing, the banker proffered his hand to shake. 'Pleased to meet you, Marshal. What brings you to these parts?'

'The Bannion brothers,' Cleary replied.

It was an answer that staggered Charles Archer.

'The Bannion brothers, you say, Marshal?' he checked. 'They're here?'

'I figure,' Cleary opined. 'Lost their tracks when the storm broke, not far from Barley's place.' He turned to Barley. 'You sure you saw no riders, Barley?' he checked again.

'Haven't seen a soul all day, Marshal,' Jack Barley lied, with an ease that he could not have only a couple of hours ago. And it troubled him that the events of those hours had in some way changed him, and not for the better.

Seth Cleary sighed. 'Come morning, I think I'll double back by your place,' he told Barley.

'Seems to me that if the Bannions were in this neck of the wood, they're probably heading for the border. My place is in the wrong direction.'

'Well,' the marshal drawled, 'my guess is that the Bannions ain't going nowhere right now. I'd bet my last dime that they're holed up around here.

'You see, Howie Bannion is one of the foxiest critters I've ever hounded. And he'd reckon that anyone dogging their trail would figure like you, Barley. And by the time their tracker would cotton on to his mistake, those Bannion boys would be long gone.'

Seth Cleary advised Archer, 'Now if I was you, Banker, I'd double check every lock on that bank of yours.' He tipped his hat. ' 'Night gents.'

'Perhaps we should postpone our business until tomorrow, Barley,' Archer suggested.

'Well . . .' Barley said thoughtfully, having to strike the right balance between disappointment and trepidation. 'I'd sure hate to make the journey back home' – he patted his shirt – 'with all this money on my person.'

He shook his head worriedly.

'If I was waylaid, we'd both be out of pocket.'

Archer tussled with the dilemma with which

Jack Barley had presented him. Hard times meant that the bank had a lot of bad debts and collateral that wasn't worth a damn as security for those loans. Among those bad debts was the Barley farm, land that the bank would have on its hands a long time, should it call in its mortgage. There was little prospect of the town prospering in the near or even medium future, and if things kept sliding the way they were, the town might fold all together.

Jack Barley let the banker stew for just the right amount of time. Then his sigh was long and weary. 'I guess I'll have to take the risk of taking this money back home, then.'

He turned and walked away.

'See you tomorrow, Mr Archer – if I've still got any business to transact, that is.'

For a time, Barley thought he had overplayed his hand, because he was gone some distance before the banker called, 'Wait up, Barley. If we're quick about this, I guess there won't be any problems.'

Barley wiped the grin from his face before he turned round and rejoined Charles Archer. He had counted on the banker's greed, rather than good sense, deciding his course of action. They continued on to the bank at a quickened pace.

'I figure the side door would be best,' Archer said, turning into an alley alongside the bank.

Can't be too careful with bank robbers about.' He stumbled over the mongrel taking sheleter in the door and angrily kicked out at the hapless dog. 'The town's full of strays,' he moaned. 'Left behind by folk leaving.'

The banker inserted the key in the lock of the side door and opened it. Jack Barley followed him inside the bank. The peculiarly musty smell of money permeated the air. On reaching his office, the bank president pulled the blinds, checking carefully that not a chink of light from the oil lamp he lit could be seen.

'OK, let's get our business concluded, Barley,' he said, briskly going to the safe to get the appropriate ledger.

Jack Barley dared not breathe. He had never set eyes on $50,000. On seeing the stacks of crisp dollar bills on the safe shelf, Barley's heart did a crazy jig. Never before had temptation come to him in such a swift torrent. The Devil was at his shoulder, whispering in his ear.

$50,000.

There for the taking.

There for the keeping.

CHAPTER ELEVEN

Archer took a ledger from the safe and placed it on his desk. 'Now, Barley,' he said, flicking open the relevant page, 'let's see the colour of your money.' When the banker looked up from the perusal of the figures, he was looking into the barrel of Jack Barley's gun.

'Sorry, Archer. This is a hold-up.' Astounded, the bank president fell back into his chair muttering incoherently. Barley explained, 'I don't have choice. The Bannion brothers are holding Ellie and Sammy hostage back at the house. And if I don't show up with that fifty thousand, they'll take their revenge on my family.'

Regaining his composure, Archer said unsympathetically, 'Your problems are yours, Barley, and none of the bank's affair. You rob this bank and you'll be an outlaw and hunted every bit as much as the Bannion brothers. And I'll damn well see to it that you are!'

'Right now there's no room in my head to think about what'll happen after. My only concern is to rescue Ellie and Sammy from the danger they're in. Now put the money in a bank sack,' he said grimly.

'And if I refuse?'

Jack Barley met the banker's challenge head on. 'If it's a toss up between your life and Ellie and Sammy's lives' – he levelled the sixgun on him – 'you'll lose, Archer.'

'Where have all those fine ideals you preached to the rest of us gone, Barley?' the banker sneered. 'When the chips are down, you're just like the rest of us.'

Jack Barley did not argue the point. In the last couple of hours he had become a man he reckoned he never could have been, because he could not say honestly, if right then and there Ellie and Sammy walked in the door free as the birds of the air, that he would not still rob the bank. His fine principles and honest dealing had brought him little by way of reward, and had left him an outcast. Because of his stubborn adherence to what he believed was right, Ellie and Sammy had suffered, too. And had his stand against the evil of war and dishonesty mattered one jot?

He reckoned not.

The bitter disappointment which hard times had been nurturing, had been finally unleashed by the Bannions' arrival. And now he knew that, in a country suffering the evils of a civil war and the greed and crimes of men who thought only of themselves, decency and uprightness were things he could no longer afford.

'Time is against me, Archer,' he growled. 'Stuff those dollars in a bank sack!'

The banker took a step back from Barley, a sudden and terrible fear in his eyes. Seeing his reflection in the glass of a bookcase behind Archer, Jack Barley saw the reason for Archer's fear. The face looking back at him was one Barley hadn't seen before. It was the face of a man who would use the gun he held. So stark and unknown was this man, that it shocked Barley.

Archer quickly stuffed the stacks of bills into a cloth sack and shoved it across the desk. Barley reached for the sack, but at the last moment hesitated, knowing that once he took possession of the sack his life would be changed forever.

Sensing his inner struggle, Archer said, 'Leave the money and walk out of here, Barley. And this will never again be spoken of. You have my word.'

'And what about Ellie and Sammy?'

'Go tell that marshal we crossed paths with about your dilemma.'

'What damn good will that do? Any sign of trouble and it'll go bad for Ellie and Sammy.'

'You take that money, and you think that a fine woman like Ellie will have anything to do with you ever again? Besides, you won't be around. You'll spend your days riding lonely trails with the law dogging your tail. And where will that leave Ellie and Sammy?'

'Don't you think I know that Ellie will hate my guts!' Jack Barley fumed. 'But I just can't let the Bannions kill her. After using her, of course.'

He grabbed the sack of bills.

'There's no other way.'

'Are you going to kill me now, Barley?'

'Kill you?' Barley exclaimed. 'That was never my plan. I'll gag you and tie you up. All I need is an hour or so to get this money to the Bannions.' As he went to do as he said, a knock on the door of the bank brought him up short. 'Not a sound,' he warned the banker. He opened the office door, and ordered Archer, 'You stand right where I can see you. Any tricks and I'll blast you.'

He went through to the bank proper and

peered out the side of the blind to see who was hammering on the front door. What he had suspected was confirmed.

The caller was Seth Cleary.

CHAPTER TWELVE

Jack Barley made quick but silent tracks back to the bank president's office. 'It's Cleary.' There was no hiding Archer's delight; a delight that was tempered by Barley's chilling warning, 'I've got nothing to lose now. So you do exactly as I say.'

'Stop this foolishness, Barley,' Archer urged. 'Slip out the side door while you still have the chance. I'll just tell the marshal that our business was finished and you left. I'll not say a word about what's gone on here.'

Jack Barley's first reaction was to accept the banker's offer and hightail it. But there was still the problem of returning to the Bannions without the money. And could he trust Archer to keep his word?

There was further hammering on the bank door.

'Time is running out, Barley.'

He could try and bluff the Bannion brothers. Tell them that the money they had obviously expected to be in the bank safe was not there. Would they believe him? Could he successfully bluff them? Bluff took the kind of liar's skill he was not practised at. Howie Bannion was as shrewd as an Irish leprechaun. If he saw through his deception, matters might get even more precarious than they already were for Ellie and Sammy. They would bear the brunt of the Bannions' spite. They'd kill him and that would be that. Ellie's fate might be a whole lot less swift and infinitely more unkind. The Bannions were savage and godless men. And what they could not take in cash, they'd take in kind.

Jack Barley decided.

'Sorry, Archer. But if I don't return to the Bannions with Ponderfoot's dollars, it'll go bad for Ellie and Sammy. And right now, their safety is my only concern.'

'Don't be a fool, Barley. Do you honestly think that once the Bannions have their hands on the money that they'll keep them off Ellie?'

The banker's blunt prediction was exactly the scenario that Jack Barley had been fighting to keep from thinking about.

'Not a damn chance, I'd say,' Archer stated mercilessly. 'If you don't want to hightail it on my terms, then have sense and take Cleary into your confidence.'

'I'll play the hand the way Howie Bannion wants it played,' Barley said doggedly. 'For him to take an interest in a peanuts bank like this, means that he's got an insider in the Ponderfoot camp who told him about Julius Ponderfoot's plans. And any tall tale I'd try to spin him would only blow up in my face.

'I've got to go back to Howie Bannion with every cent of that money, and hope that having done exactly what he wanted, I'll generate enough goodwill for him to leave Ellie and Sammy be.'

The banker shook his head. 'You're a damn fool, Barley.'

'Now' – Barley picked up the stuffed bank sack – 'I'll drop this out the window.'

Charles Archer's eyes popped with alarm. 'You'll what? You can't just drop fifty thousand dollars out the window. That's the craziest thing I've ever heard.'

'It'll only be there for a couple of minutes, until we get rid of Cleary.'

He crossed to the window, opened it, and quickly checked out the backlot. He wouldn't want a town hobo, of whom there were plenty, getting his hands on the money. He dropped the cloth sack to the ground.

Charles Archer staggered and clutched his chest, gasping for breath. Alarmed, Barley poured the banker a stiff whiskey that went a long way to reviving him, but he was still shaky when he went to admit Seth Cleary.

Jack Barley stood behind the office door, peering through the crack in the partly open door. He'd have preferred to quench the oil lamp on the banker's desk, because its backdrop glow made it more difficult to see into the gloom of the bank. But a completely dark office would seem odd when business was supposed to be in the process of being transacted. Barley silently cursed his lack of foresight. A better plan would have been for Archer to pretend that his business had been concluded and he was leaving. It was too late now to bemoan his hurried, slipshod planning.

Well, maybe Cleary would be content with not coming further than the front door.

Just before he opened the bank door, Jack Barley warned the banker, 'Everything must seem normal, or you get the first bullet.'

Charles Archer opened the bank door a crack. 'Marshal Cleary,' he greeted, his voice having none of its normal boom.

'Howdy, Archer. I was just passing. Thought I'd say hello.'

'That's mighty hospitable of you, Marshal.'

Barley winced at the sound of the banker's reedy voice. It had the kind of cracked quality that comes from a larynx constricted by fear.

'Mind if I step inside, sir?' Cleary asked.

Had the marshal picked up on Archer's fear?

'Well. . . .'

'Thank you.' Seth Cleary brushed past the banker. 'Filthy night to be standing outside.'

With no option left to him, Jack Barley stepped from behind the office door and greeted Cleary. 'Howdy, Marshal. Thought you'd be bunked down by now.'

'Early to bed ain't my bailiwick, Barley,' the lawman said, his eyes gliding over the scene. 'You gents must have a lot of business to transact.' His comments were addressed to the banker, who remained speechless.

'Oh, our business is long since concluded,' Barley said, stepping in to break the silent impasse, which was only a couple of seconds, but too long. 'Mr Archer and me were just exchanging pleasantries.'

'Mr Barley's just cleared off his debt to the bank, you see, Marshal,' Archer said croakily.

'In one go?' Cleary snorted. 'Can't have owed much.'

'No, Marshal. It was a sizeable enough sum.'

'Is that a fact?'

Jack Barley's lungs were refusing to inhale.

'I hope you won't be offended, Barley,' the lawman went on. 'But my impression was that you didn't have two dimes to rub together.'

'Barley found an unexpected buyer for his farm, Marshal.'

'That so? That's mighty good fortune in these depressed times.' Cleary said, his eyes boring into Barley.

Jack Barley wished that the banker would stop his blabbering. He also wished that he could make his excuses and leave. But that would leave Archer alone with the lawman. He'd not reach the end of the alley before Cleary would nail him.

'Local buyer?' Cleary probed.

'I can't say, Marshal. The buyer wants to remain anonymous.'

Seth Cleary's gaze went to the open bottle of whiskey on Archer's desk, from which Jack Barley had poured the banker's reviving drink only a couple of minutes before. To a whiskey-drinking man (and Seth Cleary's face showed his preference), in the main used to saloon rot-gut, the fine Kentucky Rye was to be coveted.

'Drink, Marshal?' Archer offered eagerly, glancing smugly at Jack Barley, because he was growing in confidence that time was running out for him. With Cleary obviously curious, the more time he hung around, the more questions the lawman might ask and the more curious he'd become.

'That's mighty generous, sir,' Cleary said, licking his lips as the banker poured, the warm amber of the whiskey richly reflecting the lamplight. 'The saloon's a tad rough tonight. A real ugly game of poker in progress. A young feller losing dollars he ain't got to lose, is seeing all sorts of cheating going on. Wouldn't surprise me none if there was trouble brewing.'

'Shouldn't you be preventing any trouble, Marshal?' Barley said.

'Ain't my concern. Town trouble is for the town sheriff to deal with. I dropped by his office and told him about a possible bust-up in the saloon.'

The marshal emptied his glass in one gulp.

'Pure nectar,' was his opinion. 'Now, I'd best let you gents to your business.'

'Another, Marshal?' Archer offered quickly. 'I wouldn't mind one myself.' The banker got a second glass and poured two drinks. Barley was just leaving and I'd hate to have to drink alone, Mr Cleary.'

'Don't mind if I do, sir,' Cleary said, pulling up a chair.

'I wouldn't mind a drink myself, Mr Archer,' Barley said.

'Hope you've got another bottle of this fine

brew, Archer,' Seth Cleary said, looking at the half-empty bottle the banker was pouring from.

'I didn't know you supped, Barley,' Archer said.

'Now and then,' Barley replied. 'It's a long ride back home in the storm. It'll help keep out the chill.'

Jack Barley's gaze went to the wall clock behind Archer. Alarmed, he saw that he should have started out by now to be back at the farm on time. Howie Bannion would allow a little extra time, but not much. The Bannions would be acutely aware of in whose company he had left. They'd count on him keeping his mouth shut because of the hostages they held. But each minute beyond the deadline would make them more and more jumpy. And it wouldn't take much for them to think that instead of Barley arriving back with Ponderfoot's loot, Seth Cleary might instead come riding in with a posse.

What should he do now? It looked like Cleary was settling down to finish the bottle and most of another if Archer produced one. And there was little doubt but that the banker would, if he had a bottle to hand.

He couldn't tie up and gag both men. And the only other alternative was to shoot them in cold blood. The very thought made him shudder. A bank robber he had become: a killer was a step too far. He was, in reality, left with only one option: and that was to confide in Seth Cleary.

'Marshal. . . .'

'Yeah, Barley. Got something on your mind?' he pressed, when Barley struggled to get the words out.

Jack Barley had the words just about ready to roll off his tongue when a double gun blast echoed over the town.

CHAPTER THIRTEEN

Ike Bannion was the edgier of the Bannions. 'It's way past time, Howie,' he complained.

'I can read time, Ike,' the outlaw leader growled sourly, putting the pocket watch back in his vest pocket. 'Dan is on lookout, remember.'

'We don't know this country, Howie. Might be all sorts of ways to reach this place.'

His brother had voiced Howie Bannion's concern.

'I figure we should take the woman and make tracks.'

'And leave fifty thousand dollars?' Howie snorted. 'What woman is worth that?'

'And since when is fifty thousand worth a bullet in the gut or a hangman's noose,' Ike countered. 'There'll be other banks to make good our loss. How damn long are ya goin' to wait, Howie?' he demanded angrily of his brother.

It was a question which had, as yet, no answer. Howie Bannion was trusting to instincts that had served him well in the past, and those instincts told him that Jack Barley was the kind of man who would not risk harm coming to his wife and boy. But he also knew that sooner or later, instinct, like luck, could cruelly desert a man. And there was that flicker of discontent in Barley's eyes, when he had seen the money which he had been given as bait to lure the banker, to worry about. Howie Bannion also knew that men who were as upright as saints, when faced with overwhelming temptation, sometimes went as bad as they had been good.

'I say we should hit the trail, Howie.'

Ike Bannion had not put forward a suggestion; he had laid down a challenge.

Howie Bannion held his brother's gaze, which this time did not flinch.

'If you've got more to say, say it,' the outlaw leader snarled.

Ike Bannion returned Howie's snarl. 'I think this outfit needs new leadership,' he stated bluntly. 'Cause, ya know, Brother, I reckon that you're goin' soft.'

Howie Bannion stood up from his chair. 'You figure so, Ike?' he said, with deceptive casualness, because every muscle and nerve in his body had tensed to meet his brother's challenge.

'I figure, Howie,' Ike said, settling his gunbelt on his hips, dropping the Colt pistol a couple of inches lower, the way he did when he expected gunplay as the only resolution of the problem on hand.

Howie Bannion had to admit to a grain of truth in his brother's assessment of his leadership. Of late, he had begun to tire of the endless trails he rode and the uneasy nights under skies, the stars of which were becoming progressively less attractive. He was thirty-five years old but felt ninety. The periods in the wildernesses of the West were getting longer and longer, as more and more towns became out of bounds to the gang. And either they were getting slower, or the lawmen chasing them were getting faster, but close calls were becoming the order of the day. Seth Cleary had almost nailed them, and Howie reckoned that he would have, had the storm not wiped out their sign. Cleary was only one man, of course, and they would probably have got the upper hand had a confrontation come. But the simple fact was that a couple of years ago Cleary would not have even got close. Of late, in the sleepless hours of the long nights he spent with an ear cocked for trouble, he had dreamed of a new life, maybe in Canada or across the border in Mexico. Before the war he had been a farmer like Jack Barley. Land would be cheap in Canada and Mexico. With his share of the $50,000 a Ponderfoot employee had told him about, in return for a hundred dollars to clear a bad debt to a gambler who would kill him for a single dollar, he could quit outlawry and fulfil his hankering of recent times to take a wife and plant his seed.

'Maybe we should ask Dan about that,' Howie Bannion proposed.

Ike Bannion sneered.

'Take a vote,' Howie added.

'Dan is scared of you, Howie. I ain't.'

'Maybe you should be, Ike. I'm faster than you.'

'How can ya tell?' Now that he'd finally worked up a head of steam, Ike Bannion's mood was cocky. 'You ain't never drawn agin me, Howie.'

The last thing Howie Bannion wanted was to draw on his brother. But not long ago, Ike would already be dead.

'Ever think about quittin', Ike? he asked tiredly.

'Quittin'?' Ike Bannion snorted, dismissing his older brother's question in a scoffing manner. 'To do what, Howie? Break my back 'hind a damn plough? Or maybe spend my days wipin' cow shit off my boots?'

His contempt was utter.

'See what I mean, Howie? You've gone too soft to lead this outfit.' He studied Howie Bannion. 'Maybe too soft to even be in this outfit,' he concluded.

His next offer, for a man of Ike Bannion's mean nature, was a generous one.

'You can ride out, if you want, Howie, but without a dime of the bank loot.'

Howie Bannion looked at his brother. 'I need my share as start-up cash elsewhere, Ike.'

Ike Bannion fixed his brother with a fearsome stare. 'Well, Brother, the way I see it is that you can leave with a double share, or nothin'.' He shifted his stance. 'The choice is yours.'

Before the echo of the gun blast faded, Seth Cleary was on the boardwalk outside the bank, his eyes fixed on the only possible location for the gunfire – the Lazy Dog saloon. A further shot rang out. A man clutching his gut staggered from the saloon and pitched forward into the street. The man turned towards Cleary before falling and, in the light from the saloon window, the US marshal recognized the town sheriff. Now, being the only law around, town trouble became his trouble.

Grimly, Seth Cleary headed for the saloon.

Charles Archer's soaring confidence vanished. Taking swift and full advantage of his change of fortune, Jack Barley quickly bound and gagged the banker and stuffed him in a broom closet. He took off the banker's shoes, so that kick as he might against the closet door to draw attention to his plight, his stockinged feet would not make an impression. With a modicum of luck, he'd not be found until the teller reported for duty the next morning.

Before closing the closet door, Barley apologized. 'I'm real sorry about this, Archer. But, like I said, Ellie and Sammy's safety has to come first. If I can, I'll return the money. Every cent,' he promised.

He closed and locked the closet door. Then he extinguished the lamp. There was the sound of more gunfire. Seth Cleary dealing out lead to the wrongdoer, he reckoned. He locked the main door of the bank and let himself out by the side door into the alley, locking that also. Before he left, he listened intently for the sound of any ruckus from Archer, but heard nothing.

He lost no time in reaching the backlot to retrieve the cloth sack containing the $50,000 which he had dropped out the window of Archer's office. But the cloth sack was not there! Where the hell had the sack disappeared to?

Or, rather, who had thieved from the thief?

CHAPTER FOURTEEN

Jack Barley searched in desperation. He was already way over time, which would make the Bannions' more and more edgy. However, there was no point in returning empty-handed. There was no chance that the Bannion brothers would believe that he had dropped the money out of the window at the dead of night, and it had vanished. It would sound as much of a tall tale to them, as it did to him. He swept his hands and kicked out with his boots in a circle, but found nothing. Cloth sacks didn't move on their own. Someone had to pick them up and carry them.

In desperation more than hope, Jack Barley made his way to the main street in the hope of spotting the thief. There were loud and angry exchanges coming from the saloon, but the street was deserted. Obviously the townfolk either liked to sleep through trouble, or had not the ambition left to find out what the shooting was all about. It was a town on its knees, with law and order breaking down. And poking heads often got shot off in such towns.

Barley stepped into the street, completely at a loss as to what to do next. Then, on seeing the mongrel that Archer had earlier shooed away from the bank's side door, his eyes popped: the bank cloth sack was hanging from the dog's jaws.

He had found his thief!

Ellie Barley grew ever more fearful as the angry exchanges between Howie Bannion and his brother got more bitter. It looked like there would be gunplay.

She had witnessed the growing tension between the brothers, and the fact that Jack was way overdue the time Howie Bannion had allotted him, was not calming heads. Ellie wondered where her husband had got to? Had the ruse Howie Bannion come up with tempted Archer to open the bank? It probably had; the banker, being a greedy man. Had Jack *robbed* the bank? And if he had, where was he? A sudden and awful fear gripped Ellie Barley's heart. Could he be dead?

'I think we should settle who's leader, once and for all!'

Ellie held her breath on hearing Ike Bannion's clear cut challenge to his older brother. Bannions, all of them, she could do without. But of the three, Ellie reckoned that her best chance of avoiding the awful degradation that might be her lot, lay in Howie Bannion's continued existence. Without his leash on Dan and Ike Bannion her worst fears would come to pass, of that she was certain.

Howie Bannion was no angel. But since his arrival earlier that day, she sensed a change in him. He had spoken of never having a proper family, and of his admiration for the happy Barley household, despite hard times. It had only been a brief conversation, after Ike had gone outside to the privy and Dan had been dispatched to act as lookout, but it showed a side to Howie Bannion that, nurtured, might make him a whole lot better man than he was.

'You call it, Ike,' Howie Bannion said wearily.

On impulse, Ellie stepped out of the bedroom with the absolute demand, 'There'll be no killing in my house.'

Ike Bannion sneered. 'I don't see that there's anythin' you can do about it, ma'am.'

'She's right,' Howie Bannion said. 'It'll scare the boy out of his head.'

'I ain't worried,' Ike Bannion growled.

Howie Bannion's right boot shot out and

smashed against Ike's knee. His leg buckled under him. As his hand went for his gun, Howie's boot clamped down on it and pinned it to the floor.

'We'll settle this another time, Ike!' he glowered.

'You can bet on that, Howie,' Ike growled, nursing his gun hand.

'Make some coffee,' Howie ordered Ellie.

Ellie, weak with relief, hurried to do as the outlaw leader wanted.

'Here, boy,' Jack Barley called to the mongrel.

The dog paused and looked back at the cautiously approaching figure. Used to being kicked and beaten, the dog warily eyed Barley, not sure what to expect.

'That's a good fella,' Barley coaxed.

Barley had got close enough to probably pounce. But if he mistimed his lunge, or the dog was more agile than he appeared, he'd take off and he'd never find him again.

'Watch that critter, Barley.'

Startled, Jack Barley swung around to see the town undertaker heading for the saloon, good-natured, and smiling broadly at the prospect of a couple of funerals that might just be paid for.

'That's Looper. Can be real mean sometimes.'

'Thanks for the warning,' Barley said. 'I'll sure take care.'

Having gone on a couple of paces, the undertaker paused, curious. 'Why're you trying to coax him anyway? He's just a flea-bitten hound.'

'Just took pity on him,' Barley said. 'Figured I'd take him home. Fatten him up.'

'Wasting your time, if you ask me,' was the undertaker's opinion. 'That dog's been a free-roamer for too long to settle to any chores you might have in mind for him.'

He shook his head and was about to continue, when again his curioisty got the better of him.

'What's that Looper's got in his jaws?'

'Dunno.'

'Cloth sack, ain't it?'

Jack Barley made a show of screwing up his eyes. 'Don't think so.'

The undertaker took a step closer. 'I'm sure it is. There's something in it.'

'Scraps he picked up some place, I guess,' Barley said disinterestedly. 'You know,' he bent and picked up a stone, 'I guess you're right about that dog being of no use round a farm.'

Barley was seething. Just as he had built up a rapport with the mongrel, he'd now have to stone him to prevent the undertaker from getting a closer look at the cloth sack which bore the name of the bank on it.

Just as he was about to fling the stone, Seth Cleary came from the saloon.

'You look like an undertaker to me,' he called to Josh Rawl.

'Yes, sir, I surely am.'

Rawl hurried on to the saloon, all interest in the mongrel and Barley forgotten.

'Business concluded?' the US marshal asked Barley.

'Yes, sir.'

Looper dropped the sack from his mouth. Barley's breath caught in his throat. Cleary, as of now, was too far away to see the cloth sack. But if he came any closer. . . .

'Guess I'll be moseying along.'

Barley walked to the nearest horse that was hitched to the rail outside the saloon and climbed on board, every muscle in his body strung tight with tension. The mood in the saloon had lost its rowdiness. At any second, the owner of the horse he was about to steal (having left his own hitched to a tree at the side of Archer's house), might stroll out and blast him out of the saddle as a horse-thief.

'You go carefully, Barley,' Seth Cleary cautioned. 'I'd bet my last dime on the Bannion brothers being in this neck of the woods.'

He looked towards the bank.

'Is the banker still greedily counting your dollars?'

'Naw. He's gone home.'

The marshal laughed. 'I bet he'll have sweet dreams tonight.'

Jack Barley laughed along with the lawman. 'I guess he will at that, Marshal.'

'Best get back to loose ends,' Cleary said, and turned back into the saloon.

Just to be on the safe side, Barley rode along most of the main street until the dark swallowed him up. Then he dismounted and shadow-dodged back to where Looper had dropped the sack. He grabbed it and hightailed it back along Main. The horse he'd purloined had found its way back to the saloon, used as it was to waiting long hours for its owner.

He quickly made his way to Archer's house to collect his own mount. Saddled-up, he clipped it out of town, praying that he would be on time to prevent any harm coming to Ellie and Sammy. The storm had almost passed, but it had left many obstacles in its wake: flooded creeks and fallen trees, some still smouldering after being struck by lightning. Jack Barley was conscious of time being lost, as each new impediment to his progress had to be overcome. He was also acutely aware of the danger that Seth Cleary might check on the bank. It was secured and locked up, but Barley knew that a lawman of Seth Cleary's canniness might sense that there was something amiss and investigate further.

Barley crossed the last swollen creek, raging with the torrent of water from nearby hills and canyons, a fury that almost swept him away midstream. Climbing out of the creek, he could see the flicker of light in the kitchen window of his house. From here he went on cautiously, looking for any sign of trouble and trying to gauge what he was facing into.

As he drew nearer the house, he saw Ellie pass the kitchen window carrying a coffee pot, apparently unharmed. His relief was great. Perhaps his worst fears might not come to pass. He was hoping that Howie Bannion would see the sense of hightailing it as soon as he got his hands on Ponderfoot's dollars. To achieve this, he'd tell him about Seth Cleary's keen interest in his visit to town, and the lawman's stated intention of checking back come morning.

He was about to urge the mare forward when the cocking of a pistol brought Jack Barley up short.

CHAPTER FIFTEEN

'I'll take that bank sack you've got tied to your saddle horn, Barley.'

Jack Barley turned in the saddle to face Dan Bannion, stepping from behind a tree, his cocked sixgun on him.

'I'd prefer to hand it over directly to Howie,' Barley said. 'And I reckon that he'd want it that way, too.'

Dan Bannion laughed in the skittish way he did. 'I guess big Brother would at that. But, you see, all that cash ain't gettin' nowhere near Howie or Ike.'

'So you plan to become a one-man outfit,' Barley said. 'You're loco. Howie and Ike will skin you alive.'

'They'll have to catch me first.'

'You doubt that they won't?'

'Just sling that sack over here, Barley!'

'I don't think I will,' Jack Barley said. 'If you want it' – he untied the bank sack from his saddle – 'you come and get it.'

'Then I guess I'll just have to blast you out of the saddle.'

'A gunshot in the still of night will carry far,' Barley warned. 'It'll make your brothers real jumpy.'

'I'll be long gone by the time they'll come lookin'.'

Jack Barley had the last ace in the deck to play.

'Now why have them come looking at all?' he said.

Dan Bannion's interest picked up.

'I reckon you've got a plan, Barley,' he said.

'Yeah. I've got a plan,' Jack Barley confirmed.

Seth Cleary was not sleeping well. True, the bugs in the bed were nibbling at him, but there was something else that was bothering him – a sense of unease. After some more twisting and turning, the lawman suddenly shot up in bed.

Dust!

That's what was troubling him.

More specifically, dust from the Barley attic!

CHAPTER SIXTEEN

'Barley ain't comin' back, Howie,' Ike Bannion opined. 'I figure he's got dollar-fever and ridden hell-for-leather. Or else he's caught lead and there's a posse creepin' up on us right now.'

Howie Bannion was not as certain in his rejection of Ike's fears as he had been earlier. It was now over two hours since Barley had ridden out with Seth Cleary, and he was beginning to think that he might have read the sodbuster wrong. Maybe it was as Ike said, and Barley had hightailed it. However, he was finding it difficult to believe that he would have sacrificed his wife and boy, because that would be the end result of hightailing it with Julius H. Ponderfoot's dollars.

'I don't reckon that a ghost would get by Dan,' Howie said.

That was true, Ike had to admit to himself. Dan Bannion had eyes that would spot an extra hair in a fly's eyebrow, if flies had eyebrows that is. For a brief moment that fact gave Ike Bannion comfort, until a sneaking thought shattered his new-found peace of mind.

'Maybe Dan's done a deal with Barley, Howie,' he said, in a tone barely above a whisper.

Ike Bannion's statement stunned his brother. It was a possibility he had not considered. But it might explain why Barley had not returned.

'Dan was always a tad greedy,' Ike Bannion went on. 'Maybe he figured that splittin' that fifty thousand three ways would be a cryin' shame, Howie. Dan's been sittin' his saddle uneasy in our company of late.'

Howie shook his head. 'He'd know that we'd hunt him down.'

'If we was around,' Ike said. 'Maybe Dan might just let Seth Cleary know where we are?'

'Dan would never do that.'

'Our old man would sell his sainted mother as a whore,' Ike crudely reminded the outlaw leader. 'Poison like that's got a way of being passed on. And maybe Dan got a greater big dollop of the old man's poison than even we did, Howie.

'With our necks stretched by a posse, Dan could roam free with his pockets stuffed with dollars.'

'Dan might rob us, Ike. But he'd never sell us out.'

'I wish I had your belief in our kid brother, Brother,' Ike snorted.

Howie Bannion jumped up off the chair he was sitting on and stalked across the kitchen to the window. He pressed his face close to the window to look out into the dark. Dissatisfied, he ordered Ike, 'Out the lamp.'

Ike Bannion wet his fingers and placed them on the lamp's wick. The kitchen was plunged into darkness.

'See anythin'?' Ike asked after a moment.

'Nothin'. Maybe I should ride out to find Dan.'

'Whoa now!' Ike Bannion exclaimed. 'I don't reckon that that's a very good idea, Howie.'

'Why not?' Howie Bannion snarled.

'Well, you fellas could team up. Figure that twenty-five thousand apiece is better than cuttin' old Ike in for his share.'

'Don't you trust me?' Howie barked.

'Nope.'

'Why is that?'

' 'Cause I don't trust m'self, Brother. And I'm admittin' that, for me, twenty-five thousand would be a temptation too hard to resist.'

'So have you another idea?' the outlaw leader barked.

Ike Bannion's smile was a leery one. 'I could check Dan out.'

Howie Bannion snorted. 'Who needs enemies with kin like I've got?'

'I say we take the woman and ride, while we still can,' Ike Bannion proposed.

The oldest of the Bannion brothers studied the younger. 'You want the woman real bad, don't you, Ike?'

'Well, there'll always be 'nother bank to rob, Howie.'

'There'll always be other women, too,' Howie countered.

'True, Brother. But, you see, I've got a real hot fire burnin' for this one. I'd even be pleased to take her m'self and let you and Dan have Ponderfoot's dollars.'

'That is a real hot fire you've got burnin', sure enough,' Howie Bannion said. 'But the woman stays put.'

Ike Bannion's face twisted with spite. 'You know, Howie, you're gettin' real soft inside since we got here. How come that is?'

'Don't you ever get tired of sleepin' on stony ground, Ike?' Howie Bannion asked reflectively. 'Lookin' over your shoulder every second of every day? Suspectin' ev'ryone and havin' no friends, only those doin' exactly the same thing you're doin'.

'Don't you hanker for fam'ly, Ike?'

'You've got fam'ly, Howie. Me and Dan. Or ain't we good enough no more?'

'Roots, Ike,' Howie said exasperatedly. 'Don't you want roots?'

'I'd prefer to be footloose, m'self. Apron strings and snotty-nosed brats ain't my bailiwick.' Ike Bannion laughed mirthlessly. 'Say, Howie, you wouldn't be figurin' on settin' up house with Ellie Barley, would ya?'

Howie Bannion sighed wearily. 'A woman like Ellie Barley wouldn't wipe her shoes on my back, Ike.'

'You know, Brother,' Ike said after a lengthy reflection, 'I reckon that I'm goin' to have to fight you for that woman.'

Howie Bannion did not confirm or deny the veracity of his brother's statement.

'What the heck!'

The Johnson Creek livery-keeper glared sourly at the rattling livery gate and tried to ignore the ruckus from whoever was trying to gain admittance.

'Come back in the morning,' the keeper shouted, and turned over.

'Open the damn gate,' Seth Cleary ordered. 'You lazy bastard.'

The marshal's insult was the spur needed to

prise loose the livery-keeper from his bed of straw in the livery loft. He grabbed a rifle standing against a nearby beam and slid down a rope to the livery proper.

'No man calls me a bastard,' he growled, as he swung open the livery gates.

The US marshal swung a fist. 'No man points a gun at me, day or night,' he told the dazed keeper as he struggled up off the floor. He grabbed the keeper and hauled him to his feet. 'You're lucky you're not plucking a harp right now, mister.' He shoved him aside and went to saddle his horse.

'A plan, you say?' Dan Bannion said, with a wariness born of a devious and treacherous mind. 'What kinda plan would that be, Barley?'

'The kind that will see us both ride away, richer and alive,' Jack Barley said.

'Interestin',' the outlaw commented. 'How exactly are we goin' to do that?'

Barley held up the bank's cloth sack. 'In here is one hundred thousand dollars,' he lied.

'A hun—!' Dan Bannion eyes popped and his jaw went slack.

Barley was pleased to see that the lie had, as he hoped that it would, stoked Dan Bannion's greed to a height that near stopped him breathing. And in his experience, greed made a man careless.

'Isn't that what you boys were expecting to be found in the bank safe?'

'Ah . . . sure, it was,' the outlaw bragged.

Jack Barley shook his head in wonder.

'Right up to the second that the bank safe swung open, I couldn't figure why you fellas would be bothered with a hick town bank. Then when the banker explained that all this money' – again he dangled the cloth sack tantalizingly – 'belonged to Julius H. Ponderfoot, one of America's richest *hombres*, it all made sense.

'I figure you boys bribed a Ponderfoot employee for the information, isn't that so, Dan?' he added in a friendly and wondrous manner. 'You boys are clever fellas.'

'Best hundred dollars Howie ever spent.' Dan Bannion chuckled. 'Well, he didn't actually spend it. More of a loan. 'Cause once he had the information about Ponderfoot's plans, he slit the man's throat and took his hundred dollars back.'

Jack Barley joined in Bannion's devilish mirth. 'Smart move', was his opinion.

'You still ain't explained how we're both goin' to ride away from this richer.'

'Simple,' Barley stated. 'All I need is a stake to ditch this hell-hole.' He opened his shirt to show the money Howie Bannion had given him to tempt Charles Archer to open the bank. 'And I figure that your brother Howie's dollars is that stake.'

Again, he dangled the bank sack temptingly.

'The rest is yours, Dan. Every darn dime.'

He finished, 'Deal?'

'For sure,' Dan Bannion agreed.

'Then I guess our business is done,' Barley said.

The outlaw grinned slyly. 'Yeah, I guess it is. That's one hell of a crafty plan, Barley. Never figured that an arrow-straight fella like you would think up somethin' like that.' He slapped his thigh. 'Heck, I reckon that you're in the wrong business bein' a sodbuster, Jack.'

The second long glint of mischief in Dan Bannion's eyes told Jack Barley that his charade of partnership had not been bought by the outlaw.

Dan Bannion was thinking, as soon as I've got that sack in my hands friend, you're a dead man. Casually he closed the gap between him and Barley.

Barley stood his ground, resisting the urge to widen the gap again by stepping back, giving the outlaw a hint that he had not been fooled by his show of bonhomie.

'You know,' Dan Bannion was truly puzzled, 'I never figured that you'd risk your wife and boy's lives. Ain't you worried that Howie and Ike will kill 'em out of spite when you don't turn up with the money?'

Barley shrugged disinterestedly. 'The boy's a cripple. And my wife's as cold towards me as an arctic blizzard.'

'Didn't seem that way to me,' Bannion stated. 'In fact, you two looked so cosy that Howie went kinda all soft inside.

'He figures that there was no chance that you'd take off and leave your woman and boy, even if the bank had a safe full of gold bars.'

Jack Barley laughed. 'Never figured that Howie was that dumb.'

'Well, heck. Ain't this a night of surprises.'

'What puzzles me, is why you boys took the risk of me returning with all that cash. Why you didn't rob the bank yourselves?'

'We suspected that it was Seth Cleary who was doggin' our tails, but we didn't know exactly where he was. He could've been right there on Main when we came out of the bank. Cleary's one tough bastard. He'd hit a needle standin' up straight with a bullet. There was the chance that we'd pick up lead poisonin'.'

He sniggered.

'So Howie got the bright idea of gettin' you to rob the bank. That with two thousand dollars on offer, the banker's greed would work in our favour and he'd open the bank at night. That we'd be long gone afore anyone even knew the bank had been heisted.

'Clever fella, Howie.'

'It was a smart plan,' Barley granted.

Barley lofted the bank sack towards Dan Bannion, just a tad too high for him to catch without reaching for it. He was counting on the outlaw's fear of letting the sack sail over him into the dark and the dense brush from where it could take a long time to retrieve.

Barley watched the sack sail towards the outlaw. Would he reach for it? All he had to do was glance up for a second to judge the flight of the bank sack.

Just one second. That's all he needed.

CHAPTER SEVENTEEN

Ellie Barley's unease rose in direct ratio to Howie and Ike Bannion's frustration. Thankfully, Sammy, restless at first, was now in a deep sleep. Her main concern was Ike Bannion. How long could his older brother keep him in check? There was no hiding his lust for her, and he had already backed down from one challenge to Howie Bannion's leadership. But, she suspected, with the festering mood he was in, it would not take long for him to again take issue with his brother. The next time his challenge might be covert and deadly. And that would leave her at Ike Bannion's mercy.

And what of Jack? Well over two hours had passed since he had set out for town, and there was no sign of him returning. Ellie was trying desperately to not think badly of her husband, but there was no doubt that the arrival of the outlaw brothers had changed Jack Barley in a way that she was not sure of.

She had heard Ike Bannion raise the possibility with Howie Bannion that Jack might have abandoned her and Sammy, and she was doing her utmost to find other reasons for his delay in returning. But as the minutes ticked by and there was no sign of Jack, Ike Bannion's speculation was beginning to take on a terrible reality.

Seeds of disappointment and discontent had of late been taking root in her husband, adding to the bitterness of the accident that had left Sammy a cripple, and he had begun to express doubts about the wisdom of living a life of honesty and uprightness.

'It hasn't got me anywhere, Ellie,' he had raged at the dinner-table only the previous night. 'The fact is, that no one likes a coward.'

'You're no coward, Jack,' she had told him. 'You stood for what you thought was right. And that takes a lot more courage than going along with the crowd. You live your life by the Good Book, and you'll get your reward.'

'This farm is finished, Ellie,' he had stated. 'It's time to move on.'

'To where?' she had wondered.

They had already moved three times, and

every time it had been the same when Jack's pacifist past had been revealed.

Had he done that now? Moved on? Maybe he had sensed her tiredness at always taking a stand that was at odds with the world. And maybe, too, he had seen Sammy crying too often on his return from school when he had been called a coward's son. Ellie still recalled vividly Sammy's outburst when one day such an incident had happened at class.

'Why didn't you just fight like other men, Pa?' he had railed.

And she remembered now, Jack Barley's bitter response.

'I guess you and your ma would be better off without me around, Sammy.'

After that it had been the devil's own job to get Sammy to return to class. Each morning had become fraught with him bucking against going to school.

'I guess you were right all along, Ike.' Ellie tensed on hearing Howie Bannion's resigned pronouncement. 'Barley ain't comin' back.'

Ike Bannion snorted. 'Figured him right, didn't I?'

'Yeah,' Howie Bannion conceded. 'I guess you did, Ike.'

'Prob'ly never went near town. Just took off with our damn money!' Ike Bannion's hawkish face became even more so. 'What I can't figure is, why Dan never checked back, Howie. It's been over two hours.' He snorted. 'That's if he's still waitin'. Maybe he just killed Barley and took off with the lot?'

Ellie Barley shuddered on hearing Ike Bannion raise the possibility of her husband being dead. But weep as she would if that were so, it would be preferable to Jack having betrayed and abandoned her and Sammy.

'Let's hit the trail,' Howie Bannion said.

'I'll get the woman,' Ike Bannion said, his breathlessness indicative of his lust. 'At least we'll get somethin' outa this shindig.'

Ellie Barley sprang back into the deepest shadows of the bedroom, terrified.

'Leave her be.'

'What?' Ike Bannion snarled. 'Have you gone loco, Howie?'

'If Barley's dead, or hit the trail, the boy will need his ma around more than ever,' Howie Bannion reasoned.

'That problem can be solved easily, Howie.'

Ellie heard the roll of a gun chamber.

'You'd kill the boy?' Howie Bannion asked, his tone rife with disbelief.

'Well, with the gimp dead, there'd be no reason to leave the woman behind. There'll be them long nights ahead on the trail, Howie.'

Ellie Barley listened to the long silence. She crept back to the peep from the crack in the bedroom door. Howie Bannion was standing in the middle of the kitchen, frowning thoughtfully, obviously struggling with a dilemma.

It had been a strange day. Jack Barley and Howie Bannion had been changed. Howie, Ellie reckoned, for the better; her husband, she was not sure about.

'I aim to have the woman, Howie,' Ike Bannion growled.

Ellie Barley's eyes fixed on the sixgun held by Ike Bannion. And she figured that, were Howie Bannion's decision not to Ike's liking, he'd do what he had wanted to do all along. . . .

Kill his brother.

Seth Cleary burst from the gates of the livery stable as if the Devil had set fire to his tail and pointed his horse in the direction of the Barley farm, where he reckoned the Bannion brothers were holed up. Now Jack Barley's inhospitality made sense. Not wanting any harm to come to his wife and boy, he had wanted him out of the house as quickly as possible. He cursed his dumbness in not cottoning on to the significance of the wisp of dust that had drifted past him as he had entered the Barley house – the Bannions were holed up in the loft, he reckoned. He could not have done anything about it at the time for fear of what might happen the woman and the boy. But had he understood, he could have broached the subject with Jack Barley once they had left the house, and drawn up a plan of action to flush out the Bannions. Now it might be too late. If they were still holed up, he'd prefer to be riding in on the Bannions with a posse.

Jack Barley tensed, ready to spring at Dan Bannion if he reached for the bank sack going over his head. He did. Barley sprang. He fell short. Bannion clutched the sack out of the air. Barley reached out and grabbed the outlaw's right leg and pulled. Dan Bannion was thrown backwards, but rolled out of Barley's way as he dived on him. Barley crashed heavily to the ground and made painful contact with the rotted stump of a tree, his ribs on his left side taking most of the punishment.

Dan Bannion lost no time in swinging a boot at him between the shoulders as he tried to get up. The pain already spreading out from his injured ribs joined up with the crunching pain inflicted by Bannion's hefty kick. He felt like curling up. However, he knew that Bannion would not hesitate to kill him, if not out of spite, certainly for the $2,000 stuffed inside his shirt.

He bent low, head first, and charged the

outlaw. Satisfyingly, Jack Barley felt the impact of his head with Dan Bannion's belly. He grabbed the outlaw round the waist and took him with him to crash heavily against a nearby tree. Bannion's breath was forced from his lungs. He cried out in pain. Mercilessly, Jack Barley pressed home his advantage over the weakened outlaw. Bringing his full weight to bear, he rammed the outlaw repeatedly against the tree.

Bannion managed to get a grip on Barley's hair and yanked his head back. Pain added to pain. Barley almost passed out. He was beginning to regret that he had not simply shot the outlaw. His worry was that the sound would carry to the house and alert Howie and Ike Bannion. But he'd have no such worry if Dan Bannion nailed him.

As his grip on the outlaw loosened, Dan Bannion swung a fist as hard as a hammer against the side of his head and stars exploded behind Barley's eyes. He reeled back. Bannion, at least ten years younger, recovered quickly to pace him and land another three blows, two on the face and a gut-wrencher in the belly. Hot bile piled up Barley's throat. His world spun crazily. Bannion, now sure that he had the measure of Barley, slid a hunting knife from his boot and closed in for the kill. A rage that Jack Barley never knew he was capable of boiled inside him.

He had had enough of turning the other cheek. A terrible and awesome power welled up in him, and he charged Bannion again. Taken by surprise by the power of Barley's charge, the outlaw tried to side-step him. The heel of his boot slipped off a moss-covered rock. Off balance, the outlaw wobbled right into Jack Barley's pile-driving swing. The fury of Barley's fist lifted Dan Bannion clean off his feet. The outlaw flew backwards. Barley heard a dull thud. Dan Bannion moaned, writhed, and went limp. Barley saw the blood staining the moss-covered rock where the outlaw's head had collided with it. Barley lay on the ground alongside Dan Bannion, exhausted. However, he had to find the grit to get to his feet and make it home.

Luckily the bank sack had dropped where Barley had first taken the legs out from under the outlaw. He picked up the sack and mounted up, every muscle in his body protesting. His only thought now was for Ellie and Sammy's safe delivery.

To his shame, when he had seen the inside of the bank safe, there had been a moment when he might have fallen foul of the temptation to cut and run. But now he knew that without Ellie and Sammy by his side, there wasn't treasure enough in the world to satisfy him.

*

Howie Bannion looked steadily at his brother Ike. 'We leave the woman be.'

'And if I don't agree?' Ike snarled.

Howie Bannion shifted his stance. 'Then I guess it's time to settle who's the boss of this outfit once and for all, Ike.'

CHAPTER EIGHTEEN

Ellie Barley dared not breathe. Her hope for her and Sammy's safety lay in Howie Bannion. His reputation as a notorious outlaw was justified. The Bannion brothers had a long list of cruelty and terror. However, in the last couple of hours she had witnessed a change in Howie Bannion that had set him apart from his brothers. At first, Ellie had held out little hope of surviving the Bannions' visit, but she had gradually begun to hope that she and Sammy might. Now, if Ike Bannion killed his older brother, there would be no hope. Ike would take her with him to visit all sorts of indignities on her in the lonely places a man of his kind would have to travel. And, as matters stood, Ike having a gun already in his hand, the odds of Howie clearing leather fast enough to win the duel were a thousand to one against.

Would Ike Bannion go through with his challenge this time? Or would he back off again?

Ellie looked worriedly at Sammy who had begun to toss restlessly in his sleep, his hands flaying to protect himself from some imaginary threat. Since his accident, his nightmares were many. And when he was awake, the feisty spirit that had been a hallmark of his character was slowly deserting him.

'Who wants a cripple in the way, Ma?' he'd said only the day before, when his twisted limb had become entangled with his other leg and he had pitched forward, spilling the jug of fresh milk she had given him to put on the dinner-table.

And, recently, she had had to work harder and harder to convince Sammy of his worth to her and his pa. However, with each reassurance, Sammy seemed less certain of his value.

'You call it any time you like, Ike,' Howie Bannion said.

Looking behind him from higher up on the trail to the hollow in which he had left Dan Bannion, Jack Barley thought he saw the silhouette of a rider going down the slope into the hollow. He could not be sure of the rider's identity, but the man's slouching saddle gait marked him down as Seth Cleary. All the way to town and while he was robbing the bank, he had wondered when the significance of the wisp of dust from the attic would register with the lawman. It was only a matter of time before it would, but Barley had hoped that it would not before he reached home with the money he hoped would buy Ellie and Sammy's safety.

Jack Barley quickened his pace. The moon which now dominated the sky, with only threads of the storm left, lit the trail well. But, like most sodbusters, he was far from being an expert horseman, so the faster pace he was setting held more danger for him than a ranch hand, the greater part of whose day was spent in the saddle, master of his horse and shrewd reader of terrain.

He crested a hill overlooking the house. There was lamplight in the kitchen. The house seemed to be at peace. At first his hopes rose. But on reflection he knew that the apparent peace might be down to no one being home. The thought that Ike and Howie Bannion had left with Ellie and Sammy sickened him.

He went down the slope slowly, reasoning that if Ellie and Sammy were gone, there was nothing immediate he could do about it. And if they were still in the house with the Bannions, any direct approach might spook the outlaws, because, by now, their nerves would be raw, and their trigger fingers jumpy.

He edged up to the house inch by careful inch. A distance off, he dismounted, ground-hitched his horse and went on on foot, first taking cover at the side of the house and then, crouched, slowly made his way to the lighted kitchen window.

Carefully, he peered into the room. Howie and Ike Bannion were standing facing each other – Ike holding a sixgun that was not directly aimed at the outlaw leader, but needed little adjustment to achieve that. Was he seeing the preliminaries to a gunfight? There had been signs of Ike Bannion's displeasure at Howie's leadership, but had Ike Bannion's displeasure reached the point where he was prepared to kill his own brother?

There was no sign of Ellie.

If he made his way to the side of the house where Sammy's bedroom was situated, he might be able to enter through the window. It would be a tight fit, but he might just about squeeze through. The Bannion brothers were presently preoccupied with their dispute, so their focused concentration on each other might work in his favour.

If he got inside the house, undetected, he might be able to get the drop on them. He had seldom used a gun, but tonight, should he get the opportunity, he'd not hesitate. This was no time for the kind of reasoned argument he would have engaged in only a short couple of hours ago. Now he was ready to kill Howie and Ike Bannion, and the change in him made him quake in his boots.

Arriving at the side of the house, he saw that Sammy's bedroom window was shut. Ellie was in the room, looking fearfully at Sammy tossing restlessly. Another nightmare, he reckoned. He tapped gently on the window to get Ellie's attention. Her relief on seeing him was palpable. She hurried to open the window. Barley squeezed through the open window and dropped noiselessly to the floor. Ellie clung to him. Her delight at seeing him raised Jack Barley's spirits, and made his determination to defeat the Bannions absolute.

'Is what I saw through the kitchen window for real?' he asked Ellie in a whisper.

'Yes,' she confirmed. 'Ike Bannion has challenged Howie for the leadership of the gang.'

'There is no gang anymore, Ellie. I killed Dan Bannion. And if the gunfight goes ahead, that will leave only one Bannion standing.'

He slid the ancient pistol he was packing from its holster.

'And maybe not even that,' he said grimly.

He put Ellie aside.

'Stay out of the line of fire.' He looked to the restless Sammy. 'And keep Sammy quiet.'

He made his way to the bedroom door and took in the scene in the kitchen through the crack in the door panel through which Ellie had been monitoring the situation.

'You can always back down and do this another time, Ike,' Howie Bannion proposed.

Should he wait? Jack Barley pondered. If one of the Bannions killed the other, it would only leave one to deal with. But, were Ike Bannion to accept his brother's suggestion, the tension between them would evaporate and that would mean that they're attention would refocus, robbing him of the edge he now reckoned he enjoyed.

'You still sayin' we should leave the woman be?'

'That's what I'm still sayin', Ike,' Howie Bannion stated bluntly.

'Never figured you'd go all soft-hearted, Howie,' Ike snorted. 'That's a real big surprise, and a real shame too.'

'I've met good people in this house today, Ike.' Howie Bannion's gaze was distant. 'The kind of good people we used to be before the war. And I guess that's what I want again.'

Ike Bannion laughed. 'How d'ya aim to do that, Howie, with every damn lawman wantin' to see you hanged?'

'There's got to be some place, Ike. Mexico. Canada, maybe. You could ride with me. We could break those horses we always dreamed of breakin' as kids.'

Ike Bannion snorted. 'I figure that wantin' to be folk like we used to be, is just plain dumb dreamin'. No one is goin' to let the Bannion boys reach El Dorado, Howie. At least not suckin' air. We're goin' to keep on ridin' the trail to Hell until a hangman's noose or a bullet in the gut is goin' to finally dispatch us to Satan.'

Ike Bannion's features set in stone.

'I'm takin' the woman, Howie,' he stated unequivocally. 'And if you want to stop me, you're goin' to have to draw.'

Jack Barley decided to wait until there was only one Bannion left to deal with. And maybe if Howie won, there wouldn't even be one. The Bannion elder might simply ride away, improbable as that seemed only a short time ago.

That's when Sammy's nightmare reached a pitch and he screamed out.

CHAPTER NINETEEN

Charles Archer had finally managed to manouevre himself in the tight confines of the broom closet in which Jack Barley had imprisoned him, to get his considerable bulk against the closet door. Then, his back against the door, he swung forward and back in a see-saw fashion, building up momentum each time his back connected with the door. The small, enclosed space did not permit him to use his bulk to the full to apply pressure on the door and it held for a long time, almost to the point of him giving up as his energy waned, before, in one final heave, the door frame shattered and the lock popped. He tumbled backwards out of the broom closet.

Free of his prison, the banker rolled across the bank floor to the main door to rattle it with his feet. A drunk wandering home from the saloon paused to look around him stupidly, and staggered on after his rot-gut-befuddled brain could make no sense of what he was hearing. He was at the end of the boardwalk when he paused again, a hint of reason struggling to surface through his alcoholic haze. He shuffled back to the bank, sometimes on the boardwalk, other times stumbling on to the street. He stood in front of the bank door scratching his head.

Inside the bank, Archer thought he heard the shuffle of feet outside, and began to pummel the door again. The drunk leapt back from the bank door and fell off the boardwalk. His eyes widened when he heard the banker's muffled voice. The drunk got to his feet and cautiously approached the bank door.

'Who's in there?' he asked.

More muffled sounds.

Another man coming from the saloon, only mildly inebriated, began to laugh when he saw the drunk talking to the bank door. He crept up behind him.

'Boo!'

The drunk fell backwards into the other man's arms, eyes rolling wildly. 'The bank is haunted, Ed,' he wailed.

'Sure it is, Larry.' The man called Ed humoured the drunk. His jocularity was abruptly curtailed when the bank door began to rattle furiously.

'Told ya,' Larry said smugly. Then there were more muffled sounds from the other side of the door. Larry shook his head. 'Haunted.'

'That ain't no ghost,' Ed said. 'Someone's locked in the bank!'

He went to the edge of the boardwalk and shoulder-charged the door. The bank door was blown back by the force of Ed's charge, and his momentum carried him headlong into the bank, tumbling over Archer on the floor. He quickly removed the banker's gag, who declared, 'The bank's been robbed by Jack Barley!'

'The Bible-thumper?' Ed questioned doubtfully.

'Go and fetch the US marshal in town,' Archer ordered Ed. 'A fella by the name of Seth Cleary. He's bunked down at the boarding-house at the end of Main.'

'Ain't now,' Ed said. 'Saw him riding hell-for-leather out of town a while 'go.'

'Where was he headed?'

Ed shrugged.

'Round up a posse,' the banker commanded.

Ed was shaking his head. 'A posse at this time of night?'

'I'll pay each man a hundred dollars,' Archer stated.

'A hundred dollars!' Ed yelped, his muddy eyes lighting up.

'Two hundred to the man who can organize

it,' the banker added.

'Hell, you'll get your posse, Mr Archer,' Ed promised. 'Even if I have to raise the dead!'

Ed hurried along the street hammering on doors and hollering out Archer's need and terms. In ten minutes a dozen men were mounted and ready to ride, with twice as many sour because they weren't needed.

Archer headed the posse.

'I don't give a damn if Jack Barley lives or dies,' he growled, 'as long as the bank retrieves its money.'

'I don't know why Barley bothered,' one of the posse said. 'A church collection would have more'n the plate than the bank's got in its safe.'

The banker glared at the outspoken man. 'You're out, Myers,' he barked.

'Out?' Myers growled sourly. 'I got outa bed to join your damn posse, Archer.'

'Pity you didn't button your lip when you got out of bed,' the banker growled back. 'Now clear off.'

'Ain't never goin' to put 'nother dime in your bank, for sure.'

The banker scoffed. 'You don't have a dime, Myers. Let's ride!'

'Let's have us a drink, Ben,' Larry the drunk suggested, sidling up to Myers as the posse hit the trail.

'Aw, shut up,' Myers raged, and landed a blow on the side of the drunk's head.

Larry crashed back against the saloon hitch-rail and cried out as his spine shuddered. He fell to the ground and rolled into a ball, whining.

Myers strode off.

Recognizing another loser, Looper came and sat by the drunk.

Seth Cleary rode down into the hollow, negotiating the narrowest section of the trail with the skill of a rider born to the saddle. Before becoming a lawman, he had earned a living as a bronco rider, moving from rodeo to rodeo, and had only opted for a marshal's badge when his younger brother Tom was gunned down for simply bumping into a gun-slick passing through the town he lived in, when, coming from the general store carrying a sack of flour, some of it spilled on the gunnie's new boots. There was only one argument he had ever had with Tom, and that was about his footloose ways.

'When're you going to settle down, Seth?' was the first question Tom would ask whenever they met, which was not too often. 'Put down roots and find yourself a good woman as a wife. Raise a family, Seth. That's what God intended a man to do.'

Though Tom was his younger brother, in good

sense he was years his senior.

He would argue that he was not the settling kind.

'Supper at the same time every evening, and sleeping under a roof every single night ain't my bailiwick, Tom,' he'd give as a counter argument. 'And a woman under my feet all the time would be my idea of punishment, and would be pure hell for her, 'cause root me in the one place for more than a couple of weeks at most, and I get meaner than a hungry vulture.

'As for kids. I think I've got a few round the territories,' he'd josh his brother, enjoying his despair.

Then, over supper, Tom would talk about his plans and dreams to build a ranch from the raw ground of the valley he had settled in. He'd look out at the acreage that was his, and tell Seth that one day, 'And in the not too distant future,' he'd vouch, 'this will be the Circle C ranch, Seth.'

The day he was murdered, Tom had just persuaded the bank that his dream of ranching was worth investing in. It had taken Seth Cleary two years to catch up with Tom's slayer. The desire to kill him had burned a hole in Seth's heart. But, when he finally cornered him and was about to kill him, he realized, that though revenge would be sweet, the gunning down of the killer would taint him with a poison that would change him forever, and that was not what Tom Cleary would have wanted. So, instead of gunning down Thad Blayney, he hog-tied him and delivered him up for hanging.

'You interested in becoming a lawman?' asked the sheriff he had delivered Blayney to.

He had never entertained the idea, he told him.

'This country needs law and order bad,' the sheriff had said. 'And it needs fair and good men to enforce the law, if this country is to ever lose its blood lust.'

Later that night in the town saloon, the sheriff had joined him at the bar.

'Got a vacancy for a deputy,' he murmured, between slugs of beer, and then added, 'And one day, you might even be one of those fancy US marshals.' The sheriff tagged on what he reckoned was the final selling point. 'Got a daughter of marriageable age, too, young feller.'

'Badge only,' Seth Cleary had said. 'I ain't the marrying kind, Sheriff.'

'Badge only,' the lawman agreed.

Seth Cleary was shaken from his pleasant reverie by the whack of a rifle butt in the midriff, and a second blow to the side of the face as he doubled up from the first assault. He toppled from the saddle and crashed heavily to the ground, the impact jarring every bone in his body. He looked up into the blood-caked face of Dan Bannion.

Bannion hauled the dazed marshal to a tree and tied him to it with his lariat. 'Barley thought I was done for,' he gloated. 'But he's goin' to find out different, ain't he?' He stood over the semi-conscious lawman. 'Barley first,' he said. 'Then I'll come back for you and kill you slowly, lawman.'

He chuckled evilly.

'That's if some hungry critters don't gobble you up.'

He mounted up on Cleary's horse, his own having wandered off. The horse reacted to the scent of the crusted blood on the outlaw's head and face, and the feel of a new rider in the saddle.

'You stop your antics, horse,' Bannion barked. 'Or I'll put a bullet in your head.'

As if understanding the threat, the mare settled.

Bannion laughed. 'Now that's horse sense, I reckon.' Riding up out of the hollow, the outlaw said grimly, 'I'm comin' for you, sodbuster!'

CHAPTER TWENTY

Sammy Barley's scream of terror at the demons of his nightmare, acted as a brake on Ike and Howie Bannion's confrontation. Jack Barley waited behind the bedroom door for the outlaws inevitable investigation. All he could hope for was to crack the first Bannion skull to enter the bedroom, and hope that the surprise would give him the edge over the other. He had thought about appearing, gun blasting. But if Howie was the one to buy lead, it would mean that Ike, gun already in hand, would have the advantage. Barley was acutely aware of his lack of skill with a gun. He might even miss completely. And the pistol he was depending on had been sitting in a drawer unused for almost five years. The damn thing might blow up in his face.

Ellie Barley proved to be the more quick-witted. She flung open the bedroom door. 'It's just Sammy having a bad dream. Not surprising under the circumstances,' she added feistily.

The explanation brought the Bannions up short.

'Just stop the brat's caterwaulin',' Ike Bannion growled, 'if you don't want his throat slit.'

Ellie closed the bedroom door and hurried to calm Sammy. 'Sshhh, honey,' she coaxed the terrified boy. 'The bad dream is over now.'

Sobbing and bleary-eyed, Sammy clung to her. Jack Barley came to enfold them both in his arms. When Sammy quietened down, Ellie pleaded, 'What're we going to do, Jack?'

'I think I know how we'll get the measure of the Bannions,' he said. 'But you'll have to play a role that'll not sit well with you, Ellie.'

Seth Cleary came round, cursing his carelessness. He should have anticipated trouble. He tugged at the rope binding him to the tree, but Dan Bannion had secured it well and it would take time he didn't have to work free of it, if he could.

Looking up to pinpoint the source of rustling in nearby bushes, the marshal saw two pairs of glowing eyes watching him from the dark. He heard teeth gnashing. More eyes. He could smell coyote. Cleary cut loose with a holler and thrashed his bound feet. The eyes vanished. But soon they were back. He thrashed his feet again, and again they vanished. However, the time it took before they reappeared was shorter. The third time Seth Cleary thrashed his legs, the eyes kept watching. More eyes were added. The critters could not be fooled any longer. In their wily brains they knew that the man they were watching could not fight back.

'I don't know if I can do as you want, Jack,' Ellie Barley said, her gentle face twisted in disgust at her husband's suggestion.

'I don't think I can take two of them, Ellie.'

Barley's plan was for Ellie to play up to Ike Bannion. Lure him away from his brother. He had no doubt that Ike Bannion's lust would override his good sense.

'And I'll only get one chance, Ellie,' Barley said.

'I guess I don't have a choice then,' Ellie said sombrely.

Bracing herself, Ellie left Sammy's bedroom to face the outlaws.

'How's the boy, ma'am?' The concerned question was Howie Bannion's.

'Settled,' Ellie said. 'Thanks.'

'And you, ma'am?'

'Fine.'

'I know it ain't been easy havin' us around.'

'No,' Ellie answered honestly.

'Heh, Howie,' Ike Bannion snarled. 'Ain't you got enough to worry about, 'sides them?'

'But' – Ellie strolled closer to Ike Bannion – 'I figure having you boys around has its compensations, too.' Her smile at Ike had the promise of a saloon dove, and he stared, stunned. 'You know, Ike, you're a fine cut of a man, if I may so.'

'Huh?' was Ike Bannion's dumb response.

Howie Bannion was equally taken aback. He'd have never figured Ellie Barley as the kind of woman she was now portraying herself as.

'The fact is' – Ellie came closer to Ike Bannion – 'Ike,' she purred. 'Now that my husband, that no good bastard, seems to have hightailed it, I'll be needing a man's protection.' Ellie's stomach heaved at the stench of stale sweat, beer and rotting teeth, but she kept her smile fixed and even more inviting. She ran her finger along the line of the outlaw's stubbled jaw, and let it linger on his lips. Ike Bannion shuddered and his eyes glowed lustfully. 'I think you might be just that man, Ike.'

'S-s-sure,' Ike Bannion stammered.

In a mirror on the wall behind Ike, Ellie saw Howie Bannion's quizzical face, and knew that it would not be long before the outlaw leader saw through her charade. And it pleased her that there was disapproval of her sluttish behaviour in his hooded eyes. Howie Bannion had changed a great deal from the man he was a few hours ago. And Ellie Barley took a whole lot of pride in the belief that it was the homely and caring houshold into which he had stepped, that had been the catalyst for that change.

'Told ya she was yearnin', Howie,' Ike Bannion boasted, grabbing Ellie round the waist. 'Now, honey,' he chuckled, 'if I'm the man who's goin' to protect you, don't you figure that I'm due' – his chuckle became a leer – 'some comfortin'?'

Ellie snuggled up to the outlaw. 'I reckon that's a fair exchange, Ike, darling.' She drew him with her towards her bedroom and he followed, panting like a hound picking up the scent of a bitch in heat.

'Hold it!' Howie Bannion's command had the crack of a whip.

Ellie reckoned that Howie Bannion had seen through her play-acting and Jack Barley's plan had backfired, leaving her to face a man straining at the leash to bed her, and as mean as a cornered rattler.

Ike Bannion, scowling ugly, swung round to face his brother. 'Don't stand in my way now, Howie,' he ranted.

'Can't you see what she's playin' at, you dumbhead?' Howie exploded.

'Sure I can,' Ike Bannion flung back. 'And it's makin' you as green as moss with envy, 'cause it's me she's chosen.'

Howie Bannion scoffed. 'She'd prefer to poison you than love you, Ike,' he declared.

Ike Bannion laughed dismissively, but his gaze, suspicious now, settled on Ellie.

'I figure that you have a plan to separate me and Ike, ma'am,' the elder Bannion stated.

Ellie laughed whorishly. 'Ike's right, you are jealous.'

Ike Bannion hugged her possessively. 'You can see that too, huh?'

'As plain as daylight down a mineshaft,' Ellie said, returning Ike's hug in spades. She broke away from Ike and went to the bedroom door. 'You're not going to let your brother spoil our fun, are you, Ike?'

Ellie saw Howie Bannion's eyes slide towards Sammy's bedroom, and she could almost hear the wheels turning inside his head. He could not know that Jack Barley was in the room.

Ellie figured that the outlaw leader was thinking that Sammy Barley and she had cooked up a scheme. He'd know that in some of the far-flung outposts of the territory, like the Barley farm, boys as young as Sammy could often shoot as well as any man. It would be unlikely, given Jack Barley's strong-willed application of Bible principles, that his son would be one of those boys, but could Howie Bannion risk being wrong?

'I guess you're not the man I thought you were, Ike,' Ellie Barley sighed. 'Letting your brother tell you what or what not to do.' She drifted towards Howie Bannion. 'So I guess I'll ask the boss of this outfit if he wants to take your place.'

Ike grabbed Ellie and threw her aside. She crashed heavily against the door of Sammy's bedroom and it shot inwards forcing Barley to fling himself aside from the oncoming door. He crashed against a wash basin and sent it crashing to the floor. Sammy was wide-eyed with fear.

'Damn you!' Ellie yelled at Ike. 'You've broken my porcelain wash basin!'

'I don't give a damn 'bout no basin.' Ike Bannion roared. 'When I've killed my brother, I'll slit your and the boy's throats, bitch.'

'Don't, Ike,' Howie Bannion pleaded, as his brother dived for his sixgun.

Forced to respond, the outlaw leader's gun flashed from leather and blasted in one lightning-fast move. Ike Bannion was lifted off his feet and pitched against the far wall. He slid down the wall, looking in amazement at the hole in his gut pulsing blood.

'Why'd you make me do it, Ike?' Howie wailed, going to cradle his dying brother in his arms.

'H-Howie,' Ike's eyes flashed brilliantly. 'I can see Ma, Howie. She's callin' to me.' Blood seeped from his mouth. 'I'm comin', Ma.' He reached out his hands. 'Ma, don't blame Howie. I riled him good.'

His breath came in short, staggering gasps.

'Got to go now, Howie,' he said, tears welling up in eyes that were now clouding over. He stretched out his hands. 'Gee, it's real good to see you, Ma.'

Ike Bannion gasped. His eyes fluttered and closed. Howie, his anger as volatile as an erupting volcano sprang to his feet.

'Drop the gun, Bannion!' Jack Barley barked.

CHAPTER TWENTY-ONE

Howie Bannion froze.

'Turn slowly,' Barley cautioned.

'You sure you have the guts to use that gun, Barley?' the outlaw said, on turning.

'Damn sure!' Barley growled in a voice that was strange to Ellie.

She could see that as Howie Bannion, her husband had changed, too. There was a hard edge to him she was not sure she liked very much. On the other hand, Sammy, who had come to his bedroom door was well pleased.

'You tell him, Pa,' he said proudly. 'You tell him good.'

'Come here, Sammy,' Ellie ordered the youngster, gathering him to her protectively.

'Drop the gun and kick it over here,' Barley demanded of Bannion.

'And if I don't?'

Ellie shivered on seeing the hard glint of defiance in the outlaw's narrowed eyes.

'I'll shoot you where you stand,' Barley said, in a quiet determined way that scared and surprised Ellie.

'That would be plain murder,' Howie Bannion reminded Barley. 'Murder ain't condoned in the Good Book.'

'Maybe I'm through with what the Bible says, Bannion.'

'A man can change,' the outlaw said reflectively. 'Sometimes for good. Sometimes for bad.'

'He's right, Jack,' Ellie said. 'I reckon Mr Bannion's changed for the better.'

'Ma,' Sammy protested.

'You be quiet son,' Ellie commanded. She looked directly at her husband. 'You're a good man, Jack. Kill Mr Bannion in cold blood, and you'll take the bitter regret with you to your grave.'

She swung round to Howie Bannion.

'I figure that your outlaw days are over, Mr Bannion. Am I right?'

Howie Bannion reflected for a moment, and then looked at Ike, before answering. 'I reckon they are at that, ma'am.'

'You're agreeable to walk away?' Ellie pressed him.

'Guess so.'

Ellie Barley turned back to her husband. 'I think the killing is over and done with in this house, Jack.'

'Ma, he's an outlaw,' Sammy said, pointing accusingly at Howie Bannion. 'Everyone knows that you can't trust an outlaw's word.'

For Barley, Sammy had given voice to his thoughts. If he set aside the gun, how could he be sure that the more experienced and wily outlaw would keep his word.

Ellie Barley was stunned that her husband had not readily accepted a peace. Only a couple of hours before he would have not hesitated to do so.

Howie Bannion's sigh was a world-weary one. 'Seems to me that your man ain't of a mind to listen, ma'am,' he told Ellie.

'Jack?' Ellie pleaded breathlessly.

Jack Barley saw the excited gleam in Sammy's eyes, and in that gleam he saw the seeds of change; change that would make Sammy a different man to the boy he was; change that he would have to answer to his Maker for one day.

'Guns never solved anything,' he said, and placed the little used pistol on the kitchen table.

There was a breathless and anxious pause

before Howie Bannion did the same. Ellie Barley sagged with relief when his gun joined her husband's on the table.

The window shattered and a rifle poked through, Dan Bannion grinning evilly.

'Well now,' he scoffed, 'ain't this a real brotherly get together?' His hard eyes fixed on Howie Bannion. 'Brother.'

He addressed Barley, 'Tell the boy to get the bank sack and bring it here. Any tricks and I'll blast the woman first,' he added viciously.

'Let these folk be, Dan,' Howie said.

'Ya know,' the youngest of the Bannion brothers growled, 'Ike said you were goin' soft, Howie. Well, so be it. I was gettin' tired of ridin' with you and Ike anyway. The sack,' he demanded of Barley.

He pointed the rifle at Ellie.

As the coyotes closed in on Seth Cleary, he struggled to break his bonds and free himself. There was now at least a dozen critters waiting to feast on him. Greedily, they closed the circle. One, a particularly nasty specimen, dived in to snap at the lawman's right leg. He drew his knees upwards and the coyote's jaws bit into the heel of his boot. Finding it tougher than he had expected, he howled and retreated to rejoin the pack. His obviously painful experience momentarily stymied the others' ambitions and the circle round the marshal widened. But not for long, Cleary reckoned. Their hunger and the fear of losing out on a meal, because all the time the bellies to be fed were increasing in number, would eventually have them throw caution to the wind.

He had minutes, Seth Cleary reckoned, before he'd feel jaws tearing him apart.

'My trigger finger is gettin' real itchy, mister,' Dan Bannion warned Jack Barley.

'Toss him the sack and he'll kill you anyway,' Howie Bannion advised Barley. 'All of you.'

Sammy looked to his pa for guidance.

'Go on, Sammy,' Barley told him. 'Fetch the cloth sack on the floor just inside the window, where I dropped it.'

Sammy hurried away and was back in seconds. He handed the sack to Barley.

'That sack is your bargainin' chip, Barley,' Howie Bannion warned, as he went to give it to Dan Bannion. 'Hand it over and you're done for.'

'Shuddup, Howie!' Dan Bannion roared.

'Trade,' Howie Bannion counselled Jack Barley.

'I told you to shuddup!' the youngest Bannion brother raged.

Howie Bannion ignored his younger brother's warning. 'The sack for the woman and the boy, Dan,' he bargained.

Dan Bannion looked at his brother as if he could not believe what he was hearing and witnessing. 'Have you gone loco, Howie?' he quizzed. 'Somethin' gone wrong inside your head?'

'No,' Ellie said. 'Not his head. His heart. I reckon that there was a good man waiting to break out. All he needed was a little encouragement.'

'The woman and the boy for the sack, Dan,' Howie Bannion restated.

'I hold the rifle,' Dan Bannion snarled. 'No deals.'

'In that case . . .' Howie Bannion grabbed the sack from Jack Barley and held it over the lamp on the kitchen table.

Dan Bannion watched in horror as the sack began to smoulder. 'OK! The woman and the boy for the sack.'

'Go out the back way,' Howie Bannion told Ellie. 'Take my gun. Shoot in the air when you're a safe distance away.' He told his brother. 'You stay right where you are, Dan. Or so help me I'll drop this sack on the lamp.'

'Go on, Ellie,' Jack Barley urged his wife, when she hesitated.

'I don't want to go without you, Jack,' she said.

'This is the way it's got to be, Ellie,' he said, taking her and Sammy in his arms, before repeating his order to leave. 'If anything happens to them,' he told Dan Bannion, 'I'll hunt you down and kill you.'

Dan Bannion scoffed contemptuously. 'You're talkin' out of your rear end, sodbuster.'

'I wouldn't be too sure, Dan,' Howie Bannion said. 'I figure that this whole shindig's given Barley a whole lot of grit.'

'The sack,' Dan Bannion growled.

'We wait,' Howie countered.

A couple of minutes passed before a shot rang out. Howie Bannion slung the sack to his brother, who let it go past, and Howie Bannion knew why. The sack could be retrieved after he had killed them both.

'Duck, Barley!' the senior Bannion shouted.

Not wise in the ways of treachery, Jack Barley hesitated a split-second too long, making it necessary for Howie Bannion to lunge at him, just as Dan Bannion's rifle exploded. Howie cried out, clutching at his back. Barley grabbed his pistol from the table and returned fire. A lucky shot smashed into Dan Bannion's shoulder, and he ran off howling like the hounds of hell.

Seconds later, Barley heard the sound of a

horse departing. He ran to the door and yanked it open, sending lead into the night but to no effect. As the sound of Dan Bannion's departure faded, he returned to tend to Howie Bannion. The outlaw's chest was heaving, and blood was gurgling from between his compressed lips. Jack Barley did not utter any words of hope. Howie Bannion was dying, and he knew it.

Ellie Barley rushed into the kitchen and into her husband's arms. Sammy snuggled between them. Then Ellie's gaze went to the stricken outlaw. She went and knelt beside him and took him in her arms.

'Thank you, ma'am,' Howie Bannion gasped. 'It sure feels good that someone cares.'

The outlaw's eyes flickered and closed.

Jack Barley strode to where a shotgun hung on the wall and took it down, blowing dust off it. He went to the kitchen table and took from the drawer a box of shells. Ellie looked at him as he broke and loaded the blaster.

'There's unfinished business that needs tending to, Ellie.'

'I know, Jack,' Ellie Barley said. 'I know,' she added resignedly.

Seth Cleary was tensed for the first shaft of pain as the coyotes overcame their trepidation and rushed him. A hail of gunfire scattered them as their jaws were dropping saliva on him. The marshal could not believe his eyes as the Archer led posse thundered into the hollow.

A short time later, Seth Cleary led the posse to the Barley farm and rode in on the biggest surprise of his life.

It took Jack Barley two days to finally catch up with Dan Bannion. Weakened by blood loss, his progress had become slower and slower, and the covering of his sign more slipshod. He was at a creek, pretty much spent when Barley found him.

'I need a doc badly, Barley,' Bannion pleaded. 'This hole in my shoulder's turned real nasty.'

Barley's first reaction was to show no pity, but the good nature he had lived by all of his life asserted itself, and compassion for the stricken outlaw took over. He was examining Dan Bannion's wound when the outlaw slid a knife from his boot. Jack Barley saw the glint of sun on the knife's blade just in the nick of time and rolled away from its upwards thrust. He fell back. Bannion was ready to pounce. Luckily for Barley, his shotgun was within easy reach. Its boom echoed along the creek, the water of which ran red with the outlaw's blood.

The creek's current took Dan Bannion away with the driftwood and detritus after the storm.

*

Charles Archer's jaw dropped to his chest when Jack Barley entered his office and placed the cloth bank sack on his desk.

'Every cent of Ponderfoot's dollars is there, sir,' he told the banker.

The elegantly clad man seated at the banker's desk looked up curiously at Jack Barley.

'That doesn't in any way get you off the hook for bank robbery, Barley!' Archer stated stridently. He pulled a gun from his desk drawer and held it on the unarmed sodbuster. 'You'll be breaking rocks for a long time to come.'

'There's no need for an honest man to break rocks,' the seated man said, in a deep rumbling voice. He stood up. 'Julius H. Ponderfoot, sir,' he introduced himself to Barley.

Jack Barley's eyes shot wide.

'Archer's been telling me all about your problems, Mr Barley. Seth Cleary, too, a man I have the greatest respect for, tells me that he reckons that you're an honest man. And I'd say that his opinion has just been verified.'

'But he robbed your money, Mr Ponderfoot,' the banker wailed.

'And he brought it back again, Archer.' He looked steadily at the banker. 'I'd prefer to think of the whole episode as an interest-free loan.'

'An interest-free loan!' the bank president whined in horror. 'Such an idea gives me the shakes, Mr Ponderfoot.'

Julius H. Ponderfoot put an arm round Jack Barley's shoulders. 'Mr Barley, sir,' he intoned. 'I have a proposition to put to you.'

A week later, as they rolled out of Johnson Creek to take up his new position as the manager of Ponderfoot's thouands of acres of Wyoming wheat, Jack Barley stopped in town.

Surprised that he'd want to, Ellie asked, 'Why are we stopping, Jack? I thought you'd want to see the back of this town as fast as you could?'

'I surely do, Ellie,' he said. 'But there's an old friend I want to take with me.'

Perplexed, Ellie and Sammy Barley looked at each other as he went up the steps of the saloon porch, Jack Barley not being a drinking man. They were even more puzzled when he stooped to pat the head of a mongrel, and then picked up the dog in his arms and took him back and put him on board the wagon alongside Sammy, who struck up an immediate friendship with the mongrel.

'His name is Looper, Sammy.' Jack Barley released the brake of the wagon, leaned over and spat in the town's dust. 'Let's roll,' he said.